PLAYING GAUCHE

by M. Kate Allen

Thea Press

Playing Gauche
M. Kate Allen

Thea Press
P.O. Box 24905
Tempe, AZ 85285
USA
www.theapress.org

Cover art by Andrea Dobbins.

For more about M. Kate Allen, see http://www.lifeloveliturgy.com

First printing, October 2020

ISBN-13: 978-1-7335064-3-4 (Paperback)

For Luke-Thea,
Andrea-Thea,
and Megan-Thea

~and~

For Aurora,
Crystal,
Miri-Rex,
and Mason

Chapter 1

Monday, February 15, 2016

It's been exactly three months since I was exiled to the wilderness. I need assurance that this won't be read. Instead of a paper journal, this is a computer file. Password-protected. I haven't been able to write since Mom gave me the big news. But I have to write things down—I can't go silent forever. Everything's about to change, so I might as well go back to the beginning. It was November 15, 2015.

The sky glowed rose and red as I entered the kitchen and took a seat at the breakfast table. The pale pine table gleamed as the setting sun cast her spell through the windows. My parents stood together at the sink.

"Honey, Dad and I want to talk to you for a minute," Mom said.

"What's up?" I said, yawning.

Mom sat down on the chair across from mine and twisted the white gold rings on her ring finger, avoiding my gaze. Her long, fiery-brown hair was tucked behind her ears. Her eyes met mine. Dad, who was beginning to show strands of gray in his chestnut-brown hair and beard, stood tall behind her with a hand on her shoulder. His lips were set. I sat up straight.

"What?" I said again.

"Medley, I'm pregnant."

I stared at them. My mouth hung open, but no words came out. I wiped my hands on my jeans.

"It's still early in the pregnancy, and we're not exactly young anymore, so there could be difficulties. But I'm at fourteen weeks as of Friday and the doctor says everything looks fine so far," she said.

"You found out on Friday the thirteenth?"

Mom and Dad exchanged looks.

"That's great. I'm happy for you." My words fell flat, but I kept my eyes up.

"Medley, we know this must come as a shock," she said.

"But our having a baby doesn't mean we love you any less. You're our daughter, too."

Silence settled on the room, and I could hear the ticking of the kitchen clock, like a bomb approaching detonation.

"Have you guys talked about names yet?" I asked, breaking up the clock's rhythm.

Mom looked at Dad, excitement gleaming in her eyes. "Not yet. We haven't wanted to get our hopes up. We also wanted to get your ideas when the time came."

I looked at my fingers. I picked at a hangnail. The clock ticked.

"I need to go do my homework," I said. I pulled my long black hair from my right shoulder to the other, thick strands cascading down my left arm.

"Sure. Okay, sweetie." Mom stood with me. I gave each of my parents a quick hug before heading out of the kitchen and down the hall to my room. I shut the door behind me and sat on my bed, smoothing the gray paisley quilt next to my legs. I hugged my legs to my chest and stared at my reflection in the floor-length mirror that hung on the wall across from my bed.

A girl who looked nothing like her parents stared back.

A baby?

Thursday, February 18, 2016

I smell a title coming on—Medley Blunt, Rebel Writer.

Mom is due to give birth May 15. Her belly is already out to North Scottsdale.

Everything is going to change and there's nothing I can do about it. Once they see their baby, their own flesh and blood, things will never be the same. I'm going to be a second thought to them—doesn't matter that I've been here for thirteen years, doesn't matter how much they claim to love me.

Ms. Feliz came up to me at school today. Looks like I might have a gig on the school newspaper. At least I have my words.

Ms. Feliz stopped me in the hall at school. "You're Medley Blunt, correct?"

Her hazel eyes were bright and sharp behind a pair of bedazzled glasses. A mound of thick spirals sprung from her head like creosote, and she smelled of cinnamon. We were the same height. I felt strange seeing eye to eye with someone who was years older than me. Ms. Feliz was the newspaper advisor and an eighth-grade English teacher, but I'd never had an occasion to speak to her.

"Yes, I'm Medley," I said.

"Medley, Ms. Brannon showed me a story you wrote for your English class."

I shifted my weight to my left leg and folded my arms, waiting.

"It's a really good story, and I wondered if you'd be interested in writing for the school newspaper."

I unfolded my arms. "Really?"

"Really. You have a wonderful way of weaving a narrative, and I think your writing would be an asset to the newspaper staff. We meet every Tuesday right after school for an hour. Why don't you ask your parents about it and let me know?"

She extended her right hand. I took it and we shook once. She had a firm grip; I matched it.

That night at dinner, I brought it up.

"Mom and Dad, is it okay if I join the school newspaper staff? They meet on Tuesdays after school."

Mom paused mid-bite, her spaghetti dangling loosely from her fork. "Sure, Medley-girl. What sparked your interest?"

"The newspaper advisor went out of her way to ask me. My English teacher showed her a story I wrote and she was impressed."

Dad and Mom exchanged looks, a cacophony of raised eyebrows and dimples.

"What about softball?" Dad said.

"Softball practices and games will be on Sundays and Thursdays."

Mom and Dad reached an unspoken consensus. "You can join the newspaper staff, love," Mom said.

I tracked down Ms. Feliz at school the next day and told her I wanted to join the staff.

"Wonderful! I'll see you next Tuesday after school in my classroom, room 115."

"Okay," I said. My voice was cool as fire shot up my spine.

Friday, February 19, 2016

Wow. This is unreal, so I'm just going to say it straight out: I got my first period today. I was going to the bathroom, minding my own business, when I saw something dark in my underwear. At first I thought it was diarrhea because it was really dark, but it wasn't. It smelled sharp and pungent, like something metallic. It was dried up blood.

"Mom?" I called.

I heard the patter of feet coming out of the kitchen and across the dining room.

"What is it, Medley?" she said when she was outside the door.

"Can you grab me a pad?"

"Oh my gosh," I heard her say under her breath. "All that stuff is under the sink behind the first aid kit. Just lean over and you should be able to reach it."

I opened the cupboard and reached in under the sink. There were supplies tucked in the back. I wrinkled my nose at the tampons and pulled a pad out of a canvas tote. It was wrapped in thin green plastic. The pad detached smoothly from the wrapper and I stuck it carefully in my stained underwear.

I stood and turned to flush the toilet. The toilet bowl was red. *Gross.* I flushed the toilet, pulled up my jeans—*oh my god, these are stained, too*—and washed my hands. When I opened the door, Mom was waiting for me. She had a big grin on her face. Her eyes sparkled with tears.

"Congratulations, Med. You're officially a woman. How do you feel?"

"Cramped," I said, rolling my eyes. She snorted and gave me a hug.

Mom decided to take me out to dinner, just the two of us. We both got dressed up—I put on dark blue comfy jeans, a loose white boat-necked shirt, and leather boots the color of honey. She wore a flattering red dress—loose around the middle to accommodate her burgeoning baby belly—and red lipstick to match. Taking her lead, I brushed on some mascara. She drove us to Pita Jungle in downtown Phoenix, parking near Trinity Cathedral. The breeze brushed our cheeks with blush as we wandered past the cathedral's labyrinth on our way down the sidewalk.

The host seated us next to a window that looked out onto a deck lined with rows of overhead twinkling lights. Our server brought us ice water and promised to return to take our order. Mom raised her glass. I raised mine.

"To your first day of womanhood," she said. "May you look back with fondness and look forward with fierceness."

"I'll drink to that," I said, smiling.

We clinked glasses and took a sip.

"You know, when I got my first period, I was startled," Mom said. "I didn't know what I was seeing. It took me about a day to realize I'd gotten my period. I ruined my favorite tie-dye skirt."

I guffawed, spraying water into my lap. "What did Nana say about it?"

"Oh, I think she was flustered that her little girl was growing up. Since I was the oldest, I was the first. She told me where to find everything and then gave me a hug. It was all rather awkward. I decided then that if I had any daughters, I'd celebrate the day with them. And here we are."

"Did you choose me because I was a girl?"

Mom lowered her glass and reached across the table to hold my hands.

"The social worker told us about you after you were born. We didn't have a preference. We wanted you."

"Yeah, but you knew nothing about me."

"We knew that you were going to be ours, and that was enough for us."

I looked down at my lap. My eyes grew wet and hot.

"Medley, sweetheart, look at me." When I looked up, her glistening eyes met mine.

"Sweetie, your dad and I wouldn't trade you for anything or anyone. You were perfect for us from the moment we found out we were going to adopt you."

"But now you're going to have a kid that's yours—your own flesh and blood."

"And the new baby will never, ever replace you. Do you understand that? We love you to the moon."

I wiped my eyes.

"Listen, Med, we want *you* to be as involved in the new baby's life as we are. We want you to help us raise the baby. It'll be as influenced by you as it is by us."

"But I'm almost in high school. The new baby will barely know me."

"If you leave when you're eighteen and never come back home, then maybe the baby won't know you very well. But you're not planning to leave us behind forever, are you?"

I looked out the window. Lights sparkled across the deck. No one was sitting outside tonight—it was too chilly, even in the desert.

"No, I always want to be close to you guys. That's what this is all about."

Mom dipped her head to the side until her eyes reached my lowered gaze. "You'll always be our daughter."

This time I grabbed her hands and squeezed them, hard. "I love you, Mama."

"I love you, Medley-girl."

We finished eating and ordered a dessert to share. As I was digging a fork into a generous wedge of cheesecake, I caught Mom giving me a long, serious stare, the kind that normally meant I was in trouble. I put down my fork.

"What is it? Did I do something?"

"Medley, I think we ought to have a talk."

A talk? Like the *talk?*

"Mom, I already know about the birds and the bees. We don't need to go over this."

Mom shook her head.

"I know you know, and that's not what I want to talk to you about."

She was speaking in a hushed tone now.

"I want you to know why this pregnancy is such a big deal to me."

I held my water glass to my lips, noting that she had said, "me," not "Dad and me." Goosebumps covered my arms.

"Did you know that I've been pregnant before?"

"What?" I set the glass down. "I thought you never could get pregnant."

Mom folded her hands tightly on the table and looked away. "I've been pregnant three other times," she said quietly.

"But... what happened?"

Mom examined her hands. "Your father and I found out I was pregnant almost as soon as we got married. We got married right after we graduated from ASU. Our parents hoped we would head back to Ohio to settle there after we got married, but when we found out we were pregnant, we decided to settle here instead. We thought it would be easier." She took a deep breath. "I had a miscarriage just a few weeks after I found out I was pregnant. The baby wasn't far along, but...." She inhaled sharply. Her hand covered her mouth.

Panic swelled in my gut—Mom wasn't in the habit of unraveling. She set her hand back on the table, and I clasped it between my hands.

"It's okay, honey. I want you to hear this."

She started to pull back, but I didn't let go.

"I was devastated, but a few months later, we decided to try again. And we got pregnant not long afterward. But I lost that one, too, just a few weeks after the pregnancy test came back positive." She shook her head. Her eyes were red and watery now. Tears stung my eyes.

"At that point I was a wreck. But I desperately wanted a baby—I wanted to begin a new chapter for our family. I saw doctors and they ran tests, but they couldn't find a problem. We ended up getting pregnant again about a year later, and this time, the pregnancy lasted. As each day and week passed, we felt like we were holding our breath, but we gained a little more hope with each passing moment. The longer the pregnancy lasted, the safer and healthier the baby would be. When we went for our twenty-week appointment to see if it was a boy or a girl, we were so excited—the pregnancy began to feel more real. When the nurse checked for the baby's heartbeat, though, she couldn't find one. She searched, and then she had another nurse come in to search, but they couldn't find it. The baby was there on the sonogram, but there was no movement at all. I had a doctor come in an hour later to tell me that my baby had died inside me."

A lump caught in my throat. I gripped her hands tighter.

"After that I fell into such a deep depression that I had to be hospitalized. They were able to help bring me out of the worst of the depression, but we never tried for a baby after that. I threw myself into a Master's program for library science soon afterward. I knew I'd never be able to teach English to other people's kids after I'd lost three kids of my own. I began working as a librarian at ASU, and about a year later, you came along. You were a dream come true." She looked at me, blinking tears.

"You are and always have been the best thing that's ever happened to me, Medley. And this little critter in here," she said, patting her belly, "is never going to replace you, not ever. But I want you to know that this baby matters to me exactly as much as you matter to me, and I need you to be the best big sister you possibly can be. Can you do that?"

I nodded. I got up and put my arms around her, pressing my cheek against her cheek. "I love you, Mommy. And I love the little squirt, too," I said.

"I love you to the moon, Medley-girl," she whispered.

Thursday, February 25, 2016

My period is finally over.

I've been thinking about what Mom said the other night. She talked about how things are going to be when the new baby is born. Then she told me that she'd had three pregnancies before this one, and that she'd lost them all—the third one she lost halfway through. Poor Mom. Poor Dad. I can't imagine what it must have been like for them. Three times? She asked me to be the best big sister I can be to the baby. I'm not sure what I can do when the kid isn't even here yet. But I'll do what I can. Still, even though she insists the baby will never replace me, I know that this baby will always be closer to them than me, because this baby will be their own flesh and blood. How can there be any deeper connection than that?

In other news, I'm starting softball practice next week. I played Little League for years. Last year we won the state tournament. This is the first year I'm going to be on an all-girls team and the first time I'll be playing softball. Leaving still feels unreal. It was one of the hardest decisions I've ever made. I loved my team, and I was an awesome baseball player. But after Charles Bedlam tried to force me to make out with him after we won the championship, and half the team cheered him on, there was no way I was ever going to go back. Who knew *puberty could turn guys you've known forever into raging hormonal monsters? It sucks that this is what it came to. Thank goodness for Aaron—he was the one who shoved Charles off me and threw eye-daggers at everyone else. He wishes we could still play on the same team. It helps that we're both lefties—the pitchers always have a hard time with us.*

Now I'm going to be the one having a hard time. A bunch of the girls on my new team will have been playing softball since second grade. I'm going to have to adjust to the new ball size, the new pitching style, the new timing— everything. I'm probably going to look like an amateur.

In other news, I met with Ms. Feliz for my first day on the newspaper staff the other day. She asked me what sorts of things I'd like to write about. I said I wasn't sure. She suggested that I write about the St. Patrick's Day sock hop that's coming up. Wait till she reads what I've dug up!

We passed by a colorful patch of prickly pear as we walked toward the middle school.

"I have news," I said as we walked.

"Spill it," he said, looking at me.

"I got my period."

"Umm, congrats?"

I stuck my tongue out at him.

"That's mature," he said. Then he stuck his tongue out at me.

I cackled. Then I looked over. "So what do you think? Can we still be friends?"

"Why wouldn't we be?"

"You know. Hormones. They change people."

Aaron stopped and stared at me.

"Our friendship is safe. You know I'd never be into you in a million years, even if you acted like a girl," he said.

I punched him.

"Ow." He rubbed his arm. "You're stronger than you think."

"I know how strong I am. I know you remember how hard that ball hit your glove when I lasered it to you to get that kid out at second. Charles throwing that wild pitch turned into a play of epic proportion."

"Oh, that. I forgot. You sure you're actually a girl?"

He side-eyed me, guarding his arm as his dimples deepened. We'd had this conversation a thousand times, usually after I'd complained about some idiot on the opposing baseball team shouting at me for not being in a cheerleading outfit.

"So when do you start softball?

"Practice begins next week."

"Are you ready?"

"I guess." I swung an imaginary bat through the air. "But it's going to be weird playing on an all-girls team."

"You're going to miss me."

"Yeah, I am," I said seriously.

"It'll be okay, though." Aaron kicked at some small rocks that had rolled into the sidewalk from someone's yard. Yards lined with colorful rocks were as common in Tempe as grass in the Midwest.

"We'll see. I have the jitters. I don't know how to make new friends. You're one of the only people who gets me." I ran both hands through my hair.

"It'll give you a chance to test out your social skills. You gotta learn sometime," he said.

"Gee, thanks."

"Just act like me and you'll be fine."

"Yeah, but you're naturally outgoing. I'm an introvert."

"Exactly," he said. "You don't have to *be* me. Just *act* like me. Fake it till you make it. Just pretend that it's a game and you're trying to make a play."

"Pretend it's a game?"

"Sure. That's what I do."

He tossed back his shaggy black hair, revealing well-defined eyebrows. *He could be a model someday*, I thought to myself.

It was still early morning, and the sun cast a warm glow over the neighborhood. I kicked a rock that had fallen into the road from someone's yard. It skittered clear across the road and into a storm drain.

"Did I tell you that I signed up for the school newspaper? Ms. Feliz wants me to write about the upcoming sock hop."

"Oh, yeah?"

"She told me to take whatever angle I wanted, so I've

decided I'm going to explore the holiday itself."

"Don't you think Ms. Feliz will want you to focus on the sock hop?"

I shook my head. "Who cares? All that needs to be said about the sock hop is when it's taking place. The rest can be a lot more interesting than that."

He shook his head. "I think Ms. Feliz is about to find out how out there you are."

I grinned. "Good."

Monday, February 29, 2016

It's Leap Day. It feels like a cosmic day, a day when anything could happen.

I keep going back to what Aaron said the other day—he thinks I'm going to prove to Ms. Feliz how outlandish I am. Sometimes I think all the stuff that makes me different isn't merely superficial—that it's fundamental.

I remember reading Judy Blume's book about the girl who wants so desperately to get her period. She does some crazy things in the name of fitting in. That's not me. I'm me.

That's the only person I'm going to be. The only person I can be.

So why am I comparing myself to Mom and Dad's soon-to-be-born biological child? Maybe I don't want them to discover how I don't measure up as a kid when they see how perfect their own flesh and blood is. I don't want them to ditch me like my original family did. I don't want to think they'd do that, but some deep part of me actually does think that. I can be an outsider—I've always been one—but I don't think I could handle my family overlooking me because of their new bio-baby.

All this brings me back to how I am a fish out of water wherever I go, and I wonder if I could ever possibly belong anywhere.

Chapter 2

Before we left the house, I piled my long, glossy hair into a ponytail on top of my head and secured a wide turquoise bow at the top. It was Sunday and the Hummingbirds' first softball practice was scheduled for two o'clock in the afternoon. Normally at this time on a Sunday I'd be sharing an early Sunday dinner with my parents, but we'd postponed it so I could get ready for softball. Mom drove me to Kiwanis Park. A clover of softball diamonds stood on the southern end of the park. I caught sight of other girls my age warming up on the southwest field. All of them were dressed in shimmering turquoise shirts, black form-fitting capri pants, turquoise knee-high socks, and black cleats. I could see as we drove by that a couple of the players were lefties by the leather mitts in their right hands. They would be an advantage to the team when it came to batting into right field—just like me. I glanced down at my own uniform and straightened my shirt. My hands shook a little, just like they had at the state tournament last spring. That was Little League. This was a whole new world.

"Have fun," Mom said as I opened the passenger door to her crimson Nissan Sentra and slid out. I waved goodbye, moved to the back of the car and opened the trunk, pulled out my new softball bag, and waved goodbye again as I walked down the sidewalk toward the softball diamonds.

I hooked my bag to the chain-link fence that served as a wall for the covered dugout and pulled out my mitt and my batting gloves. I tucked the gloves, lined with soft turquoise leather, into my back pocket. I trotted out to the field as I pulled my mitt onto my right hand. Scanning the infield with one hand over my eyes, I looked around for someone to warm up with. I caught sight of our coach, Marge Shannon, who had been my physical education teacher at Waverly Elementary.

"Nice to see you, Medley," she called out to me.

"Nice to see you, too, Coach," I said. She flashed a grin at me and turned her attention to the clipboard in her hand.

A black girl I'd seen at school strode up to me. "Want to

throw the ball?" she asked.

"Sure. I'm Medley," I said, taking off my glove and holding out my right hand.

"Tiffany," she said. She took off her glove—she was also a lefty, I noted—and gave my hand a firm shake. I'd seen her in science class, but she sat near the door and I sat near the windows, so we'd never talked. She was also in my homeroom, but she sat by the teacher's desk and I was closer to the back of the room. She and I jogged to line up along the third baseline, and then she threw the ball to me. I threw it back. Next to us, a pair of girls were talking back and forth to one another in raised voices while standing fifty feet apart. One of the two players was Cynthia Marshall, whom I had known and avoided like the plague since first grade. I met her on the first day of school that year. She was in the seat next to mine when I arrived, and she gave me a long look and said to our teacher, Ms. Collins (in a voice quite as loud as the one she was using now), "I don't want to sit next to *her*. Her skin looks like poo. She probably has cooties all over." I couldn't speak. I'd never been made aware of the shade of my skin till just then. I looked down and saw that I wasn't cream or light-tan like three quarters of the other kids in the room. Mom had to explain to my teacher and Cynthia's parents why I had punched her in the face that day. I was grounded for a month and forced to say sorry to Cynthia. She never accused me of having cooties after that, though. She never commented on my skin color, either. At least not to my face.

Today I turned from her and threw the ball lightly to Tiffany, careful not to strain my arm by throwing too hard too quickly. The softball felt awkward in my hand compared to the baseballs I was used to.

"I mean, like, he's cute, but I don't want to date him," Cynthia said. She threw the ball to Audrey Lester, one of Cynthia's long-time cronies. Her hair and skin were just as light as Cynthia's were.

"He adores you, though. And how can you say he's cute? He's totally hot." The ball smacked Audrey's glove, and she threw it hard back at Cynthia.

"He's not all that." *Smack.* "Besides, I have my sights set on someone amazing." *Smack.*

"What? Who?" *Smack.*

"When he's following my every footstep, you'll know," she said coyly. *Smack.* "I just have to make him notice me first." *Smack.*

I snorted. All of a sudden, the ball whizzed past my glove; I'd missed Tiffany's throw. Snickers from Cynthia and Audrey trailed behind me as I turned to run after it.

"All right, everybody, let's huddle," Coach Marge called out. I muttered a curse under my breath, picked up the ball, and jogged over to where Coach was standing. Within fifteen seconds, the whole team, thirteen strong, had formed a circle around her.

"Welcome to the first day of the spring season, ladies. Many of you know me from P.E. at Waverly." I looked around and saw that every girl but Tiffany had gone to Waverly with me. I wondered then if we had all been hand-selected to play together.

"My name is Marge Shannon, but you can feel free just to call me Coach Marge. What I want to do today is start with some fielding drills. I'll have you rotate through the nine defensive positions while I bat the ball to various parts of the field. I'm going to be looking for accuracy and speed in getting the ball back to the pitcher, who will be Cynthia Marshall." Cynthia waved and flashed a bright white smile. I caught Tiffany's gaze and rolled my eyes. She grinned and shook her head.

"Everybody ready?" The collective assent of the team rose up in a shout, and Coach Marge began calling out names and positions. I went to second base to start. Coach began hitting softballs around the diamond—first some long ones to the outfield, which required infielders to play cutoff, and then some arcing pop-ups to the infield. The first ball went to the left fielder, Rebecca Wilson, another of Cynthia's blond-haired blue-eyed cronies; Audrey, the shortstop, caught it easily. She spun and threw it to Cynthia, who threw the ball to Tiffany who was playing catcher; she had moved to the side of the plate by a few steps so Coach wouldn't get hit. The next ball required Gwennie Lightfoot, the center fielder, to run toward right field. She took a flying leap to catch the ball and hit the ground in full extension. As she scrambled to her feet, I moved to second and caught the ball when she threw it to me. I pivoted to throw the ball toward Cynthia, but my grip on the ball was awkward and the throw was, too. The ball sailed over her head. Coach dodged the ball as it crossed home plate. I punched my glove.

"That's all right, Medley. Great job, Gwennie!" Coach called. Cynthia looked back and shook her head at me. I zeroed in on Coach Marge's next hit, which went to the right fielder, one of my former classmates whose family had emigrated from Germany. Gretchen Lotz had a long, lanky body with tan skin, golden-brown hair, and matching brown eyes. She threw the ball to me and I caught it easily. I turned and gave myself a moment to get set before throwing it in to Cynthia; this time it went straight to her glove. She called out, "Might want to move a little faster next time, Blunt."

A plethora of replies came to mind, but I figured it would be better not to get tossed from practice on the first day.

At third base, a girl named Sarah Zhang with straight black hair and well-defined muscles, dropped the pop-up that came to her. Coach yelled encouragement and hit the next ball. Gwennie caught the next pop-up easily, and then it was my turn. I lost the ball in the glare of the sun and dropped it. Cynthia, watching me, tossed her hair and audibly clucked her tongue. I scrambled after the ball, which rolled to a halt about fifteen feet behind me, and threw it hard at Cynthia. This time it was on target and hit her glove with a *thwack*. Cynthia whipped around and threw the ball to Tiffany. I felt Cynthia's eyes on me, but my eyes were on Coach. Coach Marge hit the next one to the tallest player on the team, a willowy first baseman with tan skin named Luann Sizemore. She had her long blond hair shaved close to her head on one side. Luann trotted backward gracefully, caught the ball, and threw it to Cynthia, who threw it to Tiffany.

"All right, everybody, rotate positions!" Coach Marge called out a new series of names and positions. This time she placed me at catcher and sat Cynthia in exchange for Jennifer Perez. Jennifer was one of the players on my Little League team when we first started, but she had switched to softball last year. In Little League she had often played shortstop because she was wicked quick on her feet and had a strong arm. I looked at Audrey and wondered why Jennifer wasn't playing shortstop now.

The next round of hits resulted in both catches and

drops; Jennifer caught everything that came her way, showing a confidence at the pitcher's mound that rivaled Cynthia's. *I'll bet she has a pitching coach*, I mused. My heart thumped in my chest as I found my rhythm. I caught everything she sent me, and she cheered me on loudly. I smiled and slapped both my shoulders before leaning in for the next round.

Batting practice came next, and Cynthia returned to the mound. Coach replaced me at catcher with Sheila Mitchell, an emerald-eyed, curly-haired redhead whom I'd often seen with her nose stuck in a book; she had just been in the outfield. Most of the other players and I went back to the bench to put on batting gloves. I was sixth in the lineup. When I came up to the plate, I held my bat over the plate and inched backward so the meat of the bat would be in the center of the strike zone. Then I held the bat behind me with my right elbow up and reminded myself to swing straight and pivot on my feet. Cynthia's first pitch came in and looked like it would be outside. Coach called it a strike—my first strike looking. I bit my tongue and swung the bat in slow motion a couple of times. Cynthia threw another pitch and I swung at it; this time it popped off my bat and landed foul, rolling along the third baseline. Cynthia got set for her next pitch and I held my bat up behind me, waiting. In came the pitch, and I swung hard. I heard the ball hit Sheila's glove and looked behind me in disbelief.

"You were a bit early, Medley. Cynthia, give her a pitch right over the center of the plate," Coach said. My cheeks burned; Cynthia smirked and pitched the ball. This time I made solid contact; the ball sailed into the outfield, landing and rattling the fence before it stopped.

"Yes, Medley! Let's do a few more before we move on to the next batter. You've got the location—you just need to focus on timing," Coach said. I took a deep breath and got set for the next pitch. By the time my turn was over, I'd hit the ball twice and fouled out or struck out on all the rest. I was swinging the bat hard and fast, but this wasn't Little League. If today's offensive and defensive performances were any indication, I was going to have to teach myself to slow down. I walked off the field in a cloud of thought, assessing each of my swings as my bat bag weighed on my shoulders.

Later that night, Mom and Dad were huddled over the kitchen table after dinner. I went to the kitchen for a glass and then poured myself some chilled water from the fridge. Sipping from my glass, I wandered to the table and sat down at an empty chair. "What are you guys up to?" I asked.

Mom didn't look up. "We're trying to decide on a color for the baby's room," she said. In her hands she held several strips of paint samples ranging from warm browns to yellows and greens.

"We're going gender neutral," Dad said.

"What color did you use for my room when I was a baby?" I asked.

"We didn't paint your room, actually," Mom said, still staring at the color samples. "The walls started out white and we decorated with vinyl stickers of animals like bears, elephants, and monkeys. I think we had some kind of bird in there, too. A toucan, maybe?"

"So you had me in the company of wild animals?"

Mom looked up with raised eyebrows, as if a fly had just buzzed loudly past her ear.

"Did you need something, Medley?"

"Just wondering if I get to have any input on the baby's room."

"We'll see," Mom said, turning back to her color samples. I rolled my eyes, then looked at Dad. He winked at me and took a sip of his ice water.

"Are you all done with your homework?" he asked.

"Yep."

"Well, maybe you have a book or something you could read?" Mom said.

Now both of them looked up at me. Point taken. I turned on my heels, walked out of the kitchen, and walked down the hallway to my room, closing my door with a firm click. With the push of a button I turned on my small radio and tuned in to the alternative music station, where Nirvana's "Teen Spirit" was playing. I laid down in bed, ignoring the stack of library books I had checked out using Mom's employee library card at the university, and I wondered for the umpteenth time who my bio-parents were and what life would have been like with them.

I'd asked Mom and Dad about my real parents before,

and they said they hardly knew anything. All they knew was what the social worker had told them, that my real mom was a teenager and was unmarried when she had me. My real dad wasn't anywhere in the picture.

I tossed my hair back on my pillow and raised my arms to examine my skin. I was too dark to be confused for my adoptive parents' own, and I'd been given plenty of second glances throughout the years by strangers who saw me next to my parents. I began to notice the looks after the incident in first grade with Cynthia.

Softball practice replayed in my mind. My timing was off. The softballs we used in practice were also significantly bigger than baseballs, which explained why I was having trouble fielding them. Meanwhile, Cynthia Marshall did everything perfectly while she sneered at me. *What a jerk.*

I ran my fingers down my legs. I looked like I could be either Native American or Mexican in descent. Who knew? My bio-mom did, surely, but I had no way to contact her. There were lots of folks from Mexico in this area. There were also folks from all kinds of tribes all over the state. I knew next to nothing about Mexicans or Native Americans, though. I went to an elementary school that was over three quarters white. My neighborhood was mostly white. There were multiple reservations within driving distance, but I'd never been to one. We lived in a neighborhood called the Villas at Shandalay, and the walls did a great job of keeping non-pale people out. Except for me.

With a sigh I sat up and got out of bed to walk to my desk, which was flanked by two floor-to-ceiling bookcases on one side and a velvet wingback chair that had been Nana's on the other side. Stacks of library books from school, the public library, and ASU formed cairns around my room. My sock-hop piece and the notes I had taken for it sat on the right side of my desk. I saved the middle of my desk for the laptop I kept daydreaming about. My parents didn't think a preteen needed her own computer. Or a tablet. Or a smart phone. All my friends had all kinds of technology at home and in their backpacks, and I had paper. And mechanical pencils, the height of sophistication. To be fair, I did have access to the family desktop. I also had a flip-phone. Apart from phone calls, it was only good for texting.

Aaron and I also had walkie talkies that we used to whisper to each other from our back decks, which were separated by a cream-colored stucco wall, a tall, zealous bamboo plant, and a jasmine vine. We used the walkie talkies mostly when one of us was in trouble—otherwise one of us would scale the wall and hang out in the other's room, especially in the summertime when the sun blazed down on the deck, good for heating solar ovens and not much else.

I grabbed a hair tie from my desk drawer, pulled my hair back, and reviewed my sock-hop piece. I'd written and rewritten several drafts of it in my journalism notebook.

On Friday, March 18, at 6:30PM, Wolford Middle School will host its 16th annual St. Patrick's Day Sock Hop. The Multipurpose Room will be adorned with green finery, from twirled streamers to metallic clovers.

What you may not know about this sock hop is some of the significance behind the holiday itself. St. Patrick was a sixth century Christian bishop who went to Ireland as a missionary. His goal was to convert the people of the land from their belief in many local female and male deities. It is said that he drove the snakes out of Ireland. Of equal importance in Irish culture is Brigid, who as a Christian saint is the patroness of beer and as a Celtic Goddess is guardian of the flame and of poets. Brigid is celebrated during the pagan holiday, Imbolc, and the Christian holiday, Candlemas.

If you really want to get into the spirit of this year's sock hop, in addition to clovers and greenery, you may want to consider adorning yourself with flames, poetry, and frothy rootbeer mugs!

I presented the piece to Ms. Feliz the following Tuesday during newspaper staff after school, and she raised an eyebrow.

"This isn't quite what I was expecting. I've never heard of Brigid. I'm not sure the information about her really fits."

"It does," I said, meeting her eyes. "In Ireland she's just as important as St. Patrick, if not more so. If we're celebrating this Irish holiday, we might as well include the broader context of Irish cultural tradition, right?"

Ms. Feliz cocked her head. "Are you sure you're a seventh grader?"

I straightened my spine. "Yes, ma'am."

"Well, you can include this bit about Brigid." Ms. Feliz handed the sock-hop piece back to me. "I'll add this piece to the next issue of the paper. Good work, Medley."

I smiled to myself as I sat down at one of the iMacs in Ms. Feliz's room, opened a Word document, and flipped to the latest revision of my piece in my journalism notebook.

"Oh, and Medley? Based on your work here, I think your idea for a regular column would work out quite nicely in the newspaper."

I grinned. "Thanks, Ms. Feliz."

She smiled back. "No, thank you. I think this is great."

When she turned, I slapped both shoulders and began to type.

Tuesday, March 8, 2016

There's been so much going on that I haven't had time to write. Softball practice started Sunday—we practice Sundays and Thursdays, and starting a couple weeks from now we'll have games on those days. I'm glad I have that and the newspaper staff as distractions from Mom and Dad's obsession with the new baby. Mom keeps getting bigger (and happier and more distracted in equal parts), and it feels like all I'm doing is becoming a smaller part of their world. They're so preoccupied with planning....

Playing on an all-girls team is tougher than I thought. I mean, like I said, I'm glad softball's started, but right now I look like a rookie next to the rest of the players, and I'm not accustomed to that. I was one of the best players on my Little League team. I have a lot of work to do.

I turned in my piece on the sock hop today. Ms. Feliz read it over. She didn't reject it, but she did say it wasn't quite what she expected. Good news is, she approved my idea to do a regular column. I'm a writer!

Chapter 3

The next Monday, a few minutes after the final bell rang, Aaron caught up with me. We passed by a row of creosote bushes, whose five-petaled yellow flowers were just beginning to bloom.

"I have something for you," he said.

I looked at him. "What?"

He took off his backpack, unzipped it, reached inside, and pulled out a neon yellow softball. "I'm going to help you practice, starting today."

I swiped the ball away from him and tossed it in the air. A smile grew on my lips. "Where'd you get this?"

"Big Five. It's yours. Consider it an early MVP present."

"Whaaaat?"

"That's right. You and I are going to make you the MVP of your team before this season is over."

"Ha. Yeah. Like that's going to happen after the way I've started the season." I tossed the ball in the air again, higher this time. "Thanks, Aaron. You're a pal."

"I also have something I wanted to tell you."

I began tossing the ball from one hand to another. "What?"

"I'm transgender."

The ball dropped.

"You're... what?"

He stopped, too. His eyes seared mine. "I'm a girl."

Time stretched into an eternity as I beheld my best friend, who looked back at me with earnestness and—was that fear? Our conversation from the other day came back to me.

A thousand thoughts flooded my brain.

I hugged him. Her. And Aaron squeezed me tight.

"You can call me Ariela," she whispered.

I squeezed tighter, then pulled back. "Nice to meet you, Ariela."

Monday, March 14, 2016

Oh my god. Oh my god. Oh my god.

Aaron came out to me today as transgender.

I don't know how to handle this.

Aaron is transgender, and he—she—wants me to call her—HER—Ariela.

I....

I don't know what to say or think. I don't know how to process this.

I had no clue this was coming.

And I'm the only one he's—she's—told, and she doesn't want me to tell anyone else.

So now I have to go around acting like everything's normal, everything's fine, but AARON IS A GIRL NAMED ARIELA.

Seriously?

I've never known a transgender person before.

So I have to go to school and call my best friend Aaron and refer to her as "he" because no one else knows, but actually he's a she.

I'm stunned.

I think I did the right thing. I gave her a big hug. I encouraged her.

But what's going to happen when her parents find out? When my parents find out? When the school finds out?

Aaron's—Ariela's—world is about to turn upside down.

I mean, I guess it already has. But it's about to become even more so.

I can't imagine what she's going through. I can't imagine what kind of guts it took for her to come out to me.

It's actually an amazing moment. I'm proud of her. And I'm scared for her. And I don't know how I'm going to keep this to myself. But I've got to.

Wow. Just wow. My problems seem so small right now.

Between Ariela's news and worries about Coach Marge's lineup for the opening game, I was so preoccupied that I missed the door to the newsroom after school the next day. I did some research on April holidays, which this year included Jewish Passover. I made a note to ask Aaron—Ariela—about it. After newspaper staff, the only thing between me and finding out the starting lineup for our first game was time. Ariela and I went out after school on Tuesday and Wednesday to throw the softball she'd bought me. I began to handle the ball with ease, growing accustomed to its size, weight, and color. On Thursday, my classes felt like they'd been doubled in length. The end of the school-day took an eternity to arrive.

When Mom dropped me off at Kiwanis an hour ahead of my first game, I jogged, not too slow, not too fast, to the softball field. Coach Marge was about to announce about the starting lineup. Inside, my heart was thumping in my chest. Not making the starting lineup for my softball team's first game would be unthinkable. I located Tiffany and began to toss the ball with her along the first baseline, well away from Cynthia and Audrey. A few minutes later, Coach called us into a huddle.

"All right, ladies, I've got the starting lineup ready for tonight's game, complete with defensive positions, and we're going to warm up accordingly. As I call your name, head out to your defensive spot on the field."

We all held our breath, and Coach began to call out names. "First in the batting lineup will be Cynthia, pitcher.

Second will be Tiffany, third base. Third will be Luann, first base. Fourth will be Rebecca, left field. Fifth will be Audrey, shortstop. Sixth will Gretchen, right field. Seventh will be Anna, second base. Eighth will be Gwennie, center field." I squeezed my eyes shut. "Ninth will be Medley, catcher." My breath spilled out of me like a fifteen-foot wave crashing on the beach, swallowing everything in its path. *I almost didn't make it! Good grief.* I caught a glimpse at Sarah, Sheila, and Jennifer, all of whom were going to be sitting on the bench for the game tonight. Jennifer didn't look all that surprised—she was a pitcher, and she was going to play relief for Ms. Perfect herself. Sarah, however, punched her glove with her fist and kicked the dirt with her right foot. Sheila looked neither surprised nor terribly concerned. She moved to the dugout and sat down on the bench, crossing her legs and her arms.

"All right, ladies, let's move!" Coach called. I trotted to my spot behind home plate. Coach stopped me and pointed me toward a box in the dugout that had various sized catcher's masks and protective pads. I found the mask with the snuggest fit and hurried into chest, elbow, knee, and ankle pads. Cynthia was throwing practice pitches to Coach Marge when I got back to home plate. The other players were throwing the ball to one another around the field as ball players do after a successful defensive play.

"Thanks, Coach," I said. She lifted herself out of a squat and moved to the side so I could take her place. Cynthia delivered another pitch. I caught it, dropped to my knees, and threw it back. I pushed myself back into position and waited. This time she delivered the ball high. I snatched it, barely, out of the air and returned it with a zinging throw.

"Good job, Medley. Let's do about fifteen more pitches, and then I'm going to start hitting balls out to the field." Cynthia and I got into a rhythm—pitch, catch, throw, pitch, catch, throw, pitch, catch, throw. I was doing well, and Cynthia was on target. Although I didn't like her as a human, I liked that I was playing with someone who knew her stuff.

Coach gestured for us to hold up and brought a large orange bucket of softballs out to home plate. Coach began hitting the ball, and I raked my fingers through my ponytail as I waited for the ball to come back to me. Suddenly I heard a cheer go up, and I turned to see who it was.

"Medley!" someone shouted. I didn't see anyone in the bleachers at first. I turned back to the field and searched for the ball in an effort to avoid getting hit. Then came another yell, louder this time. Just then, the ball landed in Cynthia's glove and she whirled to throw it to me. I bent my knees and put my glove out straight in front of me. The ball tipped my glove, hit my shoulder, and rolled to the backstop. I rubbed my shoulder and moved toward the ball.

"Quicker, Medley, that run's coming in. Quicker!" Coach said. I sped up, grabbed the ball, and tagged home within a few steps. I handed the ball to Coach Marge, and she put her hand on my shoulder. "There will be distractions at the real game, too, Medley. You just need to tune them out, all right?"

I nodded. "You got it, Coach."

Where's the all-star focus, Medley? You're a Little League champ, and you're acting like you've never played ball! Then I looked back at the bleachers. It was Aaron—that is, Ariela—waving a sign covered in turquoise glitter that said, "GO, MEDLEY, GO!" I rubbed my shoulder again, but I couldn't help a grin. I waved, and he—she—waved back.

Coach had already hit another one out, this time to center field, when I resumed my spot next to her. Practice went on like this for the next twenty minutes, and then we all had a chance to practice batting. I grabbed my bat from my bag and leaned it against the fence. When it was my turn to bat, I approached the plate and stood with my feet planted next to it, right in the center of the box. Cynthia had switched with Jennifer by this point. She pitched and it came in low. Coach caught it and called it a ball.

"Good eye, Medley," Tiffany called from the outfield, where she and the rest of the players were standing.

Jennifer pitched again, and this time it came in high and outside. I swung and it tipped off my bat. Coach pulled another ball out of the bucket and threw it to Jennifer. Jennifer rolled the ball in her hand behind her back, nestled it in her glove, and then wound her arm quickly for the pitch. This time it came in dead center. I swung and made solid contact. Rebecca leaped for the ball as it came down along the left field line and caught it. Catcalls from the outfield—and from the bleachers—erupted.

"Just like that, Medley," Coach said.

The next pitch came in way inside, nearly glancing my elbow. I took a breath.

Jennifer got set for her next delivery. The ball came in inside again, but I moved my back foot to the outside of the box, waited a split second longer than normal, and made contact. This time it flew into right field, just shy of where the fielders were standing. Gretchen, Gwennie, and Luann nearly collided as they tried to grab it.

"Be careful, ladies—remember to call for it if you want it," Coach called. "Great hit, Medley," she said in a lowered voice. I grinned.

The rest of my time at the plate was uneventful—I got a few strikes, a few foul tips, and a few grounders. Then my turn was over, and I jogged to the outfield to stand by Tiffany in left field.

Practice ended about half an hour later, and my best friend came over and gave me a hug. "You're gonna knock their socks off, slugger," he—she—said.

"Are you staying for the game?" I asked.

"Well, if the rapture takes place between now and gametime, you and I will still be here, so I'm gonna say yes."

I rolled my eyes and shook my head, smiling. "You're a pal," I said.

My parents both showed up for the game. I stood in the dugout and braided my hair, watching the other team, the Ravens watching us. They had black cleats, black socks, white pants, black shirts, and black bows in their hair; the lettering on their uniforms was white. They looked like the fast pitch, female rendition of the Chicago White Sox.

We were the home team, so when it was time to play I put on my pads and jogged out to home plate. The first batter to approach the plate was tall—easily five foot ten. Cynthia looked unfazed. I glanced at the bleachers for our side and saw Ariela claiming a seat next to my parents. Ariela saw me looking over and waved. My parents looked my way and followed suit. I lifted my hand to wave back at them; meanwhile, the umpire called "Batter up!"

A hint of admiration swept over me after Cynthia struck

out the first three batters in short order. *This girl is good.* She even struck out the second batter looking. Her cronies whooped and smacked her butt as we returned to the dugout. Everyone gave her high fives—even me.

The Hummingbirds did much better offensively than the Ravens. Before I knew it, I was up to bat with one runner in scoring position. We had gone through the whole lineup that first inning and brought in a total of six runs. Now I was getting set at home plate with two outs. We could keep this rally going with the top of the lineup as long as I didn't mess up. No pressure, of course.

Stay in the game, I said under my breath. I eyed the opposing pitcher and gave a few practice swings. So far she'd walked three of us. All I had to do was keep my eye on the ball and save my swings for the good pitches. The first pitch came in. "Ball low," the umpire said. I gripped my bat and gave another practice swing. The next pitch came in. "Ball outside," the umpire said. The Ravens catcher got up and jogged toward the pitcher. I took the opportunity to step out of the box and look at their outfield. The outfield and the infield were both playing me inside, as if I were going to bunt.

The Ravens catcher returned to her spot behind home plate and I stepped back in the box. The pitcher took her time, so after about five seconds, I held up my hand and stepped out. She shook her head. A few seconds later I stepped back in and held up my bat, waiting. She wound up and delivered a pitch right in my wheelhouse. I cranked it, and the ball soared all the way out to the fence where it hit the ground, clanged against the metal fence, and rolled backward to a dead stop several inches away. The center fielder had played me so far in that she spent four or five seconds just getting to the ball. By the time she got the ball, turned around, and decided where she was going to throw it, the runner who'd been on second scored a run as I was sliding into third. The third baseman tagged me just as my feet and legs slid across third base. The second base umpire threw her arms out to her sides to call me safe, and the whole Hummingbirds bleacher section erupted in screaming. I double high-fived the third base-coach, a lean, ruddy Arizona State University student named Jannie, as I sucked air. "That was a slick 60-yard dash, Medley!" she said, slapping me on my safety helmet before I handed her my ankle and elbow guards. I smiled and stood on the bag, hands on my hips, and waited for the pitcher to get set.

Cynthia came up next. She hit the ball right to the feet of the center fielder, who snatched it after it hit the grass and threw it to first with surprising power. I had led off, though, and I touched home just as Cynthia crossed first base. Both umpires threw their arms out to their sides, declaring us each safe.

In the end, we run-ruled the Ravens, taking a walk-off win of twenty-one runs to one over three innings. The Ravens looked dejected as they lined up after the game, but as the teams gave each other high-fives, I met each Raven's eyes with a smile and said, "Good game."

This was going to be a victory speech, so Coach had us sit down in a circle on the grassy outfield. I sat with my legs crossed and my hands in the grass behind me, my braid swinging as sweat dripped down my back.

"Ladies, I am really proud of you," she said. "Not only for your athleticism and skill, which were beyond evident, but for your good sportsmanship throughout the game. The other team clearly struggled, and you could have rubbed it in their faces, but you didn't. This team is a class act, and that's exactly what I want to see all season—I want you to play hard, play well, and play with sportsmanship, not arrogance. Let's keep this up. Everybody up!" We stood up and put our hands into the center of the circle. Coach yelled, "One, two, three," and we all yelled, "Hummingbirds!"

Moments later, Ariela grabbed me by the torso and carried me off the field. "Time to celebrate!" she yelled. I grinned.

Chapter 4

F*riday, March 18, 2016*

What a week this has been. Aaron is now Ariela.

Let me repeat that: Aaron is now Ariela.

Also, we won our first softball game by about a million runs last night. I felt sorry for the other team, the Ravens, but man, I feel great for us. Oh, and I had an AMAZING game— the other team played me shallow and I hit the ball all the way to the fence in the first inning. They didn't play me in after that. Also, Cynthia was almost nice to me at one point—I thought I heard her say "Good job" as she walked by me after I scored a run on her sacrifice fly in the final inning. Did hell freeze over?

Maybe it did, because Aaron is now Ariela.

And the school sock hop is tonight. In an hour. And I'm going. With Ariela. Which makes me want to laugh. Because I'm going with a girl whom everyone thinks is a boy, and some people might think there's a thing between us, except there's not and never has been, and if only they knew who this "boy" really was....

All the identity revelation and gossip aside, though, I think it's going to be fun. Aaron—Ariela—and I are both going to wear green tie-dyed knee socks. She'll be in a green pair of soccer shorts, and I'll be in a skirt with a green, sleeveless top. This skirt is one of the only skirts I own, and it's a rainbow of colors, very flowy. Ariela loves it.

Man, it's really not fair, though. As a girl I can wear skirts or pants without anyone blinking an eye, but if a boy wears a skirt, everyone will clutch their pearls and make a scene.

It would be pretty amazing if I showed up in her shorts and she showed up in my skirt.

Ha. That would go well.

I told Ariela my idea as we were walking to the school for the dance. She stopped me and stared at me.

"Seriously?"

Then I felt crummy all of a sudden, like she'd caught me making light of her identity.

"I'm sorry, Ariela. It was a silly thought." *I need to be more careful with my silly thoughts from now on.*

She continued to stare at me. "No, I mean, you want to switch with me?"

I stared at her. "You actually want to switch clothes?"

"Yeah. You wear my shorts and I'll wear your skirt."

I gaped at her. "But... what if people figure it out?"

"Figure what out?"

"That you're... you're a girl."

"They'll think it's all a big joke." Ariela's eyes brightened. "Come on, let's do it. You're probably wearing shorts under your skirt anyway, right? So I'll just slip on your skirt over my shorts."

My stomach clenched. This idea sounded less and less good.

"Ariela, even if they don't find out about you... I mean, people aren't going to like it. You might get kicked out."

"And if I do, you can write about it in the school

newspaper." Ariela winked at me.

"You think Ms. Feliz would let me do that?"

Ariela gave me one of her long looks, the kind she always gave me when she thought I was edging into the realm of ridiculousness.

"Look, Medley, I'm not going to let them keep thinking I'm a boy forever. What better way to turn the tables than to change clothes for a night? It's not like I'm going to be doing it during the regular school day. This will be a fun change at a fun event."

I looked at the ground.

"Come on—please?"

I looked up. Ariela's look was one of pleading. And she wasn't one to plead for anything.

"Sure, buddy. I'll switch with you. But if they kick you out, I'm going with you."

"Deal," she said. I slipped out of my skirt then and handed it to her. She pulled it on and twirled, right there in the middle of the street. She was wearing a Fighting Irish tee from Notre Dame on top. Her face beamed as she caught sight of the skirt swishing around her. *Not unconventional. Phenomenal.* I grinned and looked beyond her to our school, which had just come into view. A heavy feeling settled into my belly, and my smile waned.

Ms. Heger, our social studies teacher, was selling tickets at the door when we arrived. She sold me my ticket first. I handed her ten bucks, and she handed me five back. Then Ariela handed her five bucks. Ms. Heger eyed Ariela up and down.

"As soon as you're properly attired, you can come in," she said.

Ariela stood her ground. "Excuse me?"

"This isn't a circus, Mr. Spieler—it's a school dance. Boys are expected to be dressed in clothing for boys, and girls in clothing for girls. When you change into something appropriate, you can go in," she said calmly.

"And since when are the rules governing what clothing a student can wear for a school dance?" Ariela asked.

Ms. Heger ignored the question. "When you're ready to comply, you may come back. Next student, please."

Ariela didn't budge. I pulled on her hand. She shook me

off.

"I want to see the rule that says I can't come in here wearing a skirt," Ariela said. Several students turned to stare.

Just then, Mr. Brantley, the principal, approached the table.

"Son, what are you wearing?" he said.

"I'm not your son, Mr. Brantley. And as you see, I'm wearing dance clothes, just like everyone else here. Ms. Heger won't sell me a ticket because she says there's some rule against boys wearing skirts."

Mr. Brantley frowned. "Son, I'm not sure what kind of game you're up to, but it ends now. Of course boys don't wear skirts. It's in our dress code."

"Since when is there a dress code for school dances?" Ariela said.

Mr. Brantley raised an eyebrow. "Whenever a dispute arises that isn't covered by the rules of our school, it's up to my discretion to make the call. And my call is that boys need to wear boy clothing, and girls need to wear girl clothing. End of story."

"You really don't think you can just make up the rules as

you go along, do you?" Ariela said. I pulled on her arm again, and again she shook me off.

"Young man, if you're not going to comply, then I'm going to have to insist that you leave," Mr. Brantley said.

Ariela folded her arms and planted her feet. She must have thrown her hip to the side, too, because the skirt swayed gently back and forth. Mr. Brantley's face turned the color of a ripe tomato and looked as if it might explode. He grabbed Ariela's arm roughly, but Ariela shook it off.

"I'll call your parents, then, and we'll see what they have to say about it." Mr. Brantley turned on his heels, and all of a sudden Ariela was gone. A five-dollar bill lay on the table in front of Ms. Heger, and the Irish rainbow blur that was Ariela disappeared through the gym door.

"Mr. Brantley!" Ms. Heger called in a high-pitched voice. He turned. I looked at him, then looked at Ms. Heger.

"Thanks for the ticket," I said, and I ran after Ariela, just escaping Mr. Brantley's reach.

To our credit, Ariela and I got in a good twenty-five minutes of dancing in the midst of all the green finery at the sock hop, evading the searching eyes of Mr. Brantley. He must have enlisted Ms. Heger's help in finding out who we were, though, because by the time he did find us, both of our sets of parents were there with him, wondering what exactly all the hullaballoo was about. When we got back out to the lobby, Ariela hugged me. "Thanks for the good time, Med," she whispered. Ariela's parents and mine stared at her wide-eyed.

"Let's go home, Aaron," her dad said.

"Come on, Medley," my mom said.

Friday, May 18, 2016, continued

Well, Ariela thought my idea was a good one. And Ms. Heger and Mr. Brantley wouldn't let her in, saying it was against the rules—and also against Mr. Brantley's good judgment—for boys to wear skirts. And when Mr. Brantley turned to call her parents, Ariela ran into the gym, and I ran in after her. Mr. Brantley didn't find us again for almost half an hour.

I mean, if you're going to begin to introduce people to the idea that you're transgender, I guess there are worse ways to do it. But as far as anyone knows, Ariela's still Aaron, and Aaron is a boy acting out for the sake of acting out. And now the "no boys wearing skirts at school dances" thing probably will be made into a rule. So what's going to happen when she really does come out? Will they still try to stop her?

I'm worried about her. I'm worried that the people who are unable or unwilling to understand her transition won't be kind to her. That they'll be cruel to her. She deserves better. She deserves to feel safe. And I don't know how to protect her from anything that's going to come her way if she continues down the path toward coming out.

It's not like she doesn't know how to take care of herself. But I still feel protective.

I don't know what's going to happen. It's probably going to get worse before it gets better.

Things were oddly calm over the next few days. My parents said nothing to me about the sock hop—they acted like nothing had happened. When I hung out with Ariela on Saturday afternoon, she said her parents had told her after the dance that her stunt wasn't worth the five bucks she spent on it, and that was it. The Hummingbirds won the second game of the season Sunday afternoon (by five runs this time). At school on Monday, the school day passed just like any other day. There were no sudden announcements over the P.A. about proper clothing for boys and girls, no pronouncements about the importance of gender conformity. On Tuesday, the only exciting thing that happened took place at newspaper staff after school, when Ms. Feliz read over what I had about Jewish Passover and said she was eager to print it.

And then, Wednesday, disaster struck. I was watching the news with my parents that night when one of the newscasters announced that the North Carolina state legislature had passed a bill requiring people to use the bathroom that corresponded with the sex listed on their birth certificate, regardless of their gender identity.

I slipped out of the living room and called Ariela from the phone in the kitchen. "Have you seen the news?"

"Nope. Should I?"

"No, don't turn on the TV. Go google 'North Carolina' on

the internet."

She didn't say anything. I listened to the tip-tap of her typing. Then I heard silence.

"What the...?"

I held my breath.

"Unbelievable," she breathed.

"I'm so sorry, A," I said.

"At least it's not in Arizona. But Arizona... this isn't exactly a forward-thinking state. We could be next."

The truth of this settled on me. This was going to be bad for a lot of people. People like Ariela.

The silence on the telephone line grew so heavy that I nearly dropped the phone. But I held on, because I needed to hang on for her. I wasn't about to abandon my best friend.

"What am I going to do?" she whispered.

I shook my head slowly. "I don't know. But I'm here for you. I promise."

A few minutes later, we said goodbye. I went to my room, shut the door, climbed into bed, and covered my head with my pillow to muffle my sobs.

Thursday morning, my alarm sounded and I thrashed at it with my left hand, my face still buried in my pillow. My fingers found the snooze button and I pressed it with a grunt. I rolled over and squinted as rays of sunlight shone brightly through the left and right sides of my cloth, cream-colored blinds. Sleeping on the east side of the house had its disadvantages. I rubbed my eyes with my right hand. Last night's news clanged in my memory, and tears welled up in my eyes. The alarm went off again, and this time I turned it all the way off and got up. My rainbow skirt from the previous Friday was on the chair I had inherited from Nana when she died back in 2010. I grabbed the skirt and sat down in the chair to pull it on. Memories of Nana reading to me in this chair during our visits to Ohio bobbed gently in the recesses of my mind. I got up, the skirt's folds swishing around me, and the memories vanished. I slid my closet door open and clawed rapidly through my shirts till I found a white short-sleeved tee with a rainbow on the chest. I held it up to myself and looked down. It would do.

After using the bathroom, I grabbed a bagel from the kitchen counter, skipped the cream cheese, and called goodbye to my parents while I scooted out of the kitchen and out the front door. Their voices were cut off by the sound of the front door shutting behind me. I waved at them through the windows of the breakfast nook as I passed by it and hurried down the driveway and down the block. A couple of minutes later, I knocked the secret knock on Ariela's front door. When Ariela opened it, her parents called a good morning to me from the other room. We left a couple minutes later, Ariela dressed in olive drab cargo pants, steel-toe boots, and a white t-shirt.

"You look like you just walked out of your bunk at Luke Air Force Base," I joked.

Aaron—Ariela—said nothing, eyeing my outfit before looking ahead.

We walked down his street together in silence. When we turned the first corner, I caught scent of yellow oleander. I plucked one of the yellow blooms from the bush, and then another. I offered the first one to Ariela, but she waved it off. I held both of the flowers up to my nose and inhaled deeply. Their perfume was sweet and mellow, and the blooms were soft as roses. Apart from orange blossoms, the small white flowers that bloomed for a scant two weeks in February and March, these were my favorite flowers of springtime.

School came into view many steps and a good deal of silence later. As we approached the main doors, dozens of kids got off buses and streamed inside. Ariela looked ahead at the crowd and said, "You didn't have to wear that."

"The whole school should be wearing this."

A corner of Ariela's mouth crept up. Then she gave me a noogie.

"Dude, you're messing up my hair!" I protested, swatting her hands away. And then she gave me a hug.

Ariela and I parted ways to head to our homerooms as I smoothed my hair. When the bell rang, Channel 1, a student-focused news station, came on. HB2 was the first story of the day. I leaned forward to listen. As the story went on, I heard a couple of snickers behind me. I ignored them and kept listening to the story. Then I heard "Dumb faggots."

Oh, no, you didn't.

I turned. It was Charles Bedlam.

"What did you just say?" I frowned.

"Aw, look, she's wearing rainbows. I didn't know you were a dyke, Blunt."

"I haven't given it a whole lot of thought, to be honest. But talking to you sure illustrates the appeal of being one."

Charles looked at his buddy, Ron Greenfield, and snickered. "She probably is a lesbo. No wonder I don't like her."

My eyes narrowed. I got up and stood right in front of Charles, who was leaning back in his chair, legs splayed.

"You wanna learn about real men, Blunt? I could teach you something," Charles said in a low voice. He reached up to touch the waistband of my skirt and slipped two fingers inside it.

In a moment he was doubled over, groaning and squealing like a pig that'd just been trapped, and I was back in my seat, lightly massaging my knee.

"Medley and Charles, both of you get up here now, please," Mr. Irwin said. Simply dressed in khakis and a cotton button-up shirt, he was a tall, thin man with long, wavy brown hair and bright green reading glasses, which he now peered over with wide eyes.

I stood, smoothed my skirt, and walked up to Mr. Irwin's desk. I turned. Charles was still hunched over his desk, and Ron was patting him on the back.

"What happened?" Mr. Irwin asked finally, even though Charles hadn't come up to his desk yet.

I turned back to face Mr. Irwin.

"Charles appears to be incapacitated," I said.

"And when I heard his noise of protest, you were the one hovering over him. What is this about?"

"This is about him learning some manners, sir."

Mr. Irwin glanced at Charles, then back at me. He sighed and removed his glasses, rubbing the bridge of his nose. "And since when are you the one designated to teach him manners?"

"Since he decided to put his hand on me without my permission, sir."

Mr. Irwin looked back at Charles, who was breathing heavily and grabbing his crotch. Then Mr. Irwin looked back at me, as if he were trying to figure out what to do. Just then, the bell rang.

I followed Mr. Irwin's gaze to Charles, who was now

scooting out the door. He sighed.

"I trust that if there is a problem again, you will tell me rather than playing Dirty Harry."

"Dirty Harry, sir?"

Mr. Irwin shook his head. "Let me handle discipline in this room. If I catch you taking matters into your own hands again, I won't be so lenient. Got it?"

"With all due respect, sir, if Charles Bedlam puts his hands on me without my consent again, I won't be so kind."

Charles and Ron and most of the rest of the kids in homeroom were gone when I returned to my desk. I grabbed my things and headed for the door. As I exited the room, I felt a hand on my shoulder and flinched. It was Tiffany.

"I'm not normally a fan of that kind of thing, but I think Charles got just what was coming to him," she said.

I relaxed. "Thanks."

"I heard what you said to Charles. Do you know someone who's... you know?"

I nodded.

She nodded back. "I have an aunt who is. She's had a

hard time her whole life, especially since she came out a few years ago. She was married at the time, and her now ex-husband didn't take kindly to her self-revelation." Tiffany looked at the floor.

I lowered my voice. "Did he hurt her?"

"He tried to fix her--by forcing himself on her."

My mouth dropped open.

Tiffany shook her head and looked at the ceiling, then back at me. "I wouldn't let that jerk get away with touching me, either. My parents are self-proclaimed pacifists and that's what they've always taught me to be, but I'm not just going to stand there and take it while some jerk crosses the line."

I eyed the muscular curve of Tiffany's arms and legs, appreciating a strength in her that I hadn't previously perceived. "Well, I mean, we are softball players. We know how to handle balls that need handling, don't we?"

Tiffany's eyes rounded, and she burst into guffaws that rang through the emptying hallway. She wiped tears from her eyes. "I think you and I understand one another, sister friend," she said.

Just then, the bell rang.

"Oops," we said in unison. We both waved and then scurried off in opposite directions to our first period classes. I reached the door to my social studies class just as Ms. Heger was closing the door.

"You're late, Ms. Blunt," Ms. Heger said as I slid in the door. She wore a navy-blue dress suit. Her skirt's hem came just below her knees. She also wore a string of wide white pearls that matched the shade of her straight teeth. Her auburn hair, unblemished by stray grays, was pulled back in a French twist. Her perfume, whatever it was, wasn't cheap—subtle, but unwilling to go unnoticed. I gave an apology and hurried to my seat.

"Next time it will be a detention," she said smoothly— and loudly—as she clicked past me in her navy-blue pumps on the way to her desk.

"Thank you for clarifying, ma'am," I said. Several students around me snickered; others gaped.

She turned, extended her shining chrome pointer, and tapped the whiteboard with it. "State Rights" was written there in flawless cursive. "Today we're going to talk about state rights, or the right of states to govern locally. What would be an example of the opposite of local government?"

Johnny Williams, a tall, skinny boy who sat in the front row with sandy blond hair cut close and gelled back so it never moved, raised his hand, revealing the long sleeve of a button-down white shirt. Johnny had taken to wearing bow ties this year, and I wasn't sure I'd ever seen him wear the same one twice. Today's was red with white polka dots. "The opposite of local government would be national or federal government, which is sometimes referred to as 'big government.'"

"Correct. Well done, Mr. Williams. 'Big government' has another connotation. Can anyone tell me what it is?"

Johnny's hand shot in the air again. I sat back in my seat and folded my arms.

"Yes, Mr. Williams?"

"'Big government,' in addition to meaning the opposite of local government, can refer to the bloating of politicians in the federal government asserting their influence over public policy as well as the regulation of the private sector."

Ms. Heger smiled. I rolled my eyes again.

"That's correct, Mr. Williams, thank you. Now, our founding fathers, seeking relief from the oppressive big government of England, designed a constitution that would create a republic, a land of many states that would govern themselves according to the needs of the local people."

I sat forward and raised my hand. "Excuse me, Ms. Heger, but a monarchy, however oppressive it might be, wouldn't technically qualify as 'big government,' right? I mean, it was run by one king."

Ms. Heger held her pointer in both hands. Her eyes glittered, narrowing.

"According to the first definition of 'big government' Mr. Williams gave, monarchy absolutely qualifies as big government—it is the opposite of local government."

"But there were local levels of governing as well—there was a whole hierarchy of royalty and nobles beneath the king that oversaw the king's lands, yes? I mean, obviously everyone had to fall in line with the king in a way that one doesn't necessary with top politicians in a democracy, but there were also decisions that the king never needed to know about. So decisions were made at both levels," I interrupted.

"First, Ms. Blunt, the common people in eighteenth century England had no authority to elect officials who represented their interests."

Fair point. I nodded.

"The question here," she continued, "is how much authority the upper echelons of government should have over local communities. Imperialism failed with King George III, who reigned in England when the United States of America was born, and the remnants of imperialism have always been destined to fail here. The founding fathers recognized the virtues of allowing local communities to govern themselves according to their own needs, and that model of government continues today."

Ms. Heger turned her gaze from me to the rest of the class. "Can anyone think of an example of the triumph of local government over big government?"

Johnny's hand shot up again.

"Yes, Mr. Williams."

"In North Carolina, a law was passed yesterday at the state level requiring transgender people to use the bathroom of the gender recorded on their birth certificate."

"Sex, not gender," I muttered.

Ms. Heger and Johnny looked at me. Others turned their heads toward me as well.

"Ms. Blunt?" Ms. Heger asked.

"Gender is a social construct that develops throughout childhood and adult life and cannot be identified at birth. Sex has to do with one's body parts and is what doctors and nurses identify at birth." I knew this because I'd spent several hours at the library at ASU researching transgender identity, LGBTQ identities, and the difference between gender and sex in particular after Ariela told me she was a girl.

Ms. Heger took several steps toward me. My eyes met hers as she drew closer. "There are many reputable scholars and scientists who would argue that there is no significant distinction between gender and sex, Ms. Blunt," she said. "In any case, that's beside the point. We're here to talk about government. Clearly, in the example Mr. Williams chose, the people of North Carolina saw a need, and they met that need by creating a new law for their state. Other states might have different needs, so their laws might look different. That is the beauty of local government: the local people are able to govern themselves."

"I'm pretty sure the local transgender people of North Carolina would disagree that they were governing themselves when HB2 passed," I said.

"If you want to speak, you must raise your hand and wait to be called on, Ms. Blunt."

I unfolded my arms and raised my hand. Ms. Heger ignored it and continued her speech on the virtues of local government. I interrupted again.

"Being ignored by the powers that be," I said, warming to the subject, "is the danger of governance by local government alone." All eyes were on me now. "The desires of those who uphold the status quo in a small community may trample the needs of the marginalized, in part because there's no one in power at a local level to offer a challenge to the way things are. That's where so-called 'big government' can help, because eyes at the federal level may have a greater sense of perspective than a local government. The diverse needs of a whole country can bring fairness and justice to all that a state government might ignore, as we saw yesterday." I shot a look at Johnny and went on. "The more representatives there are in government, the more likely that the diverse concerns of all people will be addressed."

"Ms. Blunt, perhaps you would like a visit to the principal's office, since you have no regard for the rules of decorum in this classroom."

"Just look at Brown vs. Board," I continued, raising my voice. "The Supreme Court, stepped in with local laws that were unjust. Local government is not the be-all and end-all. Sometimes, like with this new North Carolina law, local governments are just plain wrong and need to be held accountable. It's called checks and balances, Ms. Heger."

Ms. Heger swung her pointer in my direction. With her finger, she pointed to the door.

"To the office. Right now."

I picked up my backpack, twirled around to give my

rainbow skirt a billowed effect, and walked out. A collective "Ooooh!" reached my ears, and Ms. Heger told everyone to quiet down. *Medley, one. Heger, none.*

When I arrived at the principal's office, the secretary asked for my name, instructed me to wait, called the principal, and murmured unintelligibly into the phone. I waited. The principal opened his door and gestured for me to come in nearly thirty minutes later. When I looked up, I had just finished an engrossing chapter of a Chris Crutcher novel.

"What brings you here, Medley?" Mr. Brantley said. Instead of sitting behind his desk in his leather chair, he sat on one of the corners of his desk, inches away from me. I dug my heels into the tile floor and slid the flimsy plastic chair away from him.

"Ms. Heger and I had a disagreement about the virtues of local government."

"I'm sure a difference in worldview is not what brought you to my office, Medley. Why don't you tell me what really happened?"

I stared at him in silence, my hands folded in my lap.

"I stated views that were different than hers. She wouldn't call on me when I tried to explain myself, so I spoke without permission."

"Ah. You spoke without permission."

"She told me I couldn't speak unless I raised my hand, and then she refused to call on me when I did raise my hand, even though she let another kid before me answer three questions in a row."

"And that is her right as a teacher."

"It's not her right to silence a student who's disagreeing with her in a reasonable way."

"It is indeed her right to manage her classroom as she sees fit. Your job as a student is to respect the rules each teacher has set in place so that the classroom environment is safe, friendly, and productive."

"It seemed very productive to me until she silenced me and then sent me to the office."

Mr. Brantley inched closer to me. I moved my chair again. This time I hit the wall behind me.

"Medley, I'm not sure we really understand one another

here, so let me explain it to you again. In this school, the teachers are in charge. Students are never in charge, no matter how smart or right they may think they are. You follow the rules, or you face the consequences. Right now, I think a detention this afternoon would serve you well."

"No can do, Mr. Brantley. I have a softball game after school."

"Ah. Well, perhaps you'll remember that the next time you decide to take matters into your own hands."

I began to protest, but he held a finger to his mouth.

"Are you ready to return to Ms. Heger's class now?" he asked.

Just then, the bell rang.

"No, thank you," I said.

I was out the door before Mr. Brantley could respond.

Thursday, March 24, 2016

North Carolina's lawmakers are nuts. They've just passed a law—HB2—that bans transgender people from using the bathroom that matches their gender. They're going to try to make them use the bathroom that goes with the sex on their birth certificate.

As if coming out as transgender isn't hard enough! This law is going to fan the flames of homophobia across the country. LGBTQ people are going to get hurt. People who might otherwise be overlooked might be pummeled in public places. They might even die.

Jesus.

Oh, and don't even get me started on my social studies teacher, Ms. Heger. And the principal, Mr. Brantley, defender of tyrannical teachers. I missed my softball game because of the two of them. Brantley told me to spend detention—which I did not deserve—writing an essay about the importance of recognizing the authority of teachers and other school officials. That was fun, actually—I wrote a bunch of the crap that they might say and ended it with, "So sayeth Mr. Brantley." It was a work of art. Anyway, I think I need to take this to the next level. Maybe I can sneak something into the school newspaper.

I got in a fight today. Charles Bedlam made a comment

about "faggots" during the Channel 1 story on HB2. I stood to confront him, and he grabbed at my waist while he was leering at me and calling me names—so I kneed him where it would hurt. Mr. Irwin called us up, but Charles was having a bit of trouble after first contact. As soon as the bell rang, he was out the door. Coward.

Tiffany came up to me afterward and said she supported me. I like her. She doesn't say a whole lot—she'd rather study people, I think—but I suspect that her gears are turning by the dozens all the time. Her eyes are like wells, rich and dark brown, and depths as vast as universes within them. We had a good laugh after Charles fled. Bet his buddies don't let him live that down.

Ariela told me the Hummingbirds lost today—she went to watch even though I wasn't there so she could tell me about it. Sarah, my sub, dropped a catch to home that would have ended the game—two runs subsequently scored at the top of the inning and the Hummingbirds couldn't come back offensively in the bottom of the inning, so we lost. I would have caught that final out and ended the game. Dang.

Heger and Brantley are jerks.

That Sunday was Easter, and I woke to the smells and sounds of sizzling bacon. I stretched in the morning light, willing myself out of bed with eyes still half-closed. I ran my fingers through my hair to get the night-time knots out as I shuffled out of my bedroom and down the hall. In the kitchen, Dad was wearing purple cotton pajamas and tan slippers. He opened the oven door, and the smell of cinnamon buns greeted me. My mouth watered, and I swiped a piece of bacon from the plate where several perfectly browned pieces were cooling on a paper-towel covered plate. Mom was already sitting at the breakfast table, the New York Times outstretched so I could only see the top of her head.

Mom picked up her mug to take a sip. I peered over the rim. Herbal tea, not coffee. And Mom loved her coffee. *Man, being pregnant must be a pain.*

"Have you checked your Easter basket?" Dad asked.

I turned. "I haven't had an Easter basket since I was ten," I said. I walked back to the stove to swipe another piece of bacon. As Dad was slathering icing on the cinnamon rolls with a butter knife he paused long enough to point the knife toward the living room without looking up. *Fine, I'll bite.*

I walked into the living room and found my old Easter basket in the center of the coffee table. Inside was a bed of green paper Easter grass and a package wrapped in several layers of tissue paper. "What's this?" I called. No answer. I opened it carefully where the paper had been taped. A medium sized hardcover book was inside.

I opened the book and flipped through it. It was a baby book. I flipped open the front cover and saw my name written inside. Mom's handwriting.

I sat at the table next to her. Dad came over to the table with the plate of cinnamon rolls dripping with icing that he had prepared. Mom put two on her plate and sidled up next to me so we were touching. She raised her eyebrow in the direction of the baby book.

I set down the cinnamon roll as I chewed my first big bite, and then I wiped my hand on my PJs before opening the baby book.

My mind wandered as I traced the words on the pages.

"La la loo, la la loo," I sang in soft tones. My voice had developed into something beautiful, in part thanks to Nana, who had recorded lullabies for me on CD when I was a baby to help me sleep. She was the only one who could ease me from a crying fit into a deep slumber when I was small. I sang lullabies together with her when I was a toddler, and as I grew she taught me other songs—haunting songs, songs that lingered long after she was gone.

I sang my favorite lullaby at her funeral. Everyone there cried as I sang to her. I had hoped with a secret hope that singing might wake her up, might bring her back; that she would give me a big hug and sing me to a deep calm again. It didn't happen like that.

Nana, I miss you.

Chapter 5

I woke early on Sunday, April 3, the Sunday after Easter. Soft orange morning light blanketed my room. I had just dreamed about playing a game in which Cynthia was at bat while I was catching. She flung the bat at me after her hit. It knocked the wind out of me. Now I could hear Dad's voice talking rapidly, and Mom was crying. I scrambled out of bed, opened my door, and hurried down the hall. In the dining room, I froze: Mom, laying on a towel on the tile floor, writhing.

"Mom?"

She winced and clutched her belly before letting out a moan. The receiver of the phone clicked into its handset, and Dad rushed out of the kitchen, past Mom and me, and into their bedroom. "Medley," he said in a clipped voice, "your Mom and I need to go to the hospital. The ambulance is on its way."

Bright red blood soaked through Mom's soft gray pants

and onto the towel beneath her. Just then, I heard doors slam outside. I could hear heavy boots clomp up the walkway. Dad opened the main door and the security door before they could pound on either one.

"She's in here," he said. Three paramedics came inside and set up a gurney in our dining room. Two of them, a short twenty-something muscular woman with auburn hair in two French braids and a tall bald twenty-something guy whose arms were covered in tattoos, lifted Mom onto the gurney. The third paramedic, a trim forty-something with graying blond hair checked her pulse before attaching a blood pressure cuff to her arm. They asked her questions in low tones as she cried out. Before I knew it the three of them were rolling her out.

"Lock the door behind me, Medley," Dad said. "Call me if you need me."

And then I was alone. The bloody towel lay at my feet, red and soaked with the odor of iron. I stared at it, my heart pounding. I picked it up by the corners, bagged it in a new trash liner, and placed it gingerly in the garbage pail in the garage. I checked the floor where the towel had been, and there was a dull red splotch turning brown as it dried. I grabbed a roll of disinfectant wipes from under the kitchen sink, doubled them up, and began to wipe down the floor. Many wipes later, my arms ached and my hands trembled. I deposited the bloodied wipes in a plastic bag and put them in the garbage with the soiled towel. Then I went to the bathroom, and washed my hands under water so hot that the pale side of my hands turned bright pink. The burning sensation couldn't take my mind off my mother. I turned the water off. I shook as I pressed each side of my hands against the hand towel next to the sink.

My hair was kinky from sleeping on it. I pulled it up roughly in a teardrop and threw on some jeans and a gray racer-back shirt. Then I stepped out of the house, locked the door, checked the door to make sure it was secure, and walked around the block to Ariela's. *Normal. Just pretend everything's normal.*

Ariela answered the door when I rang the doorbell.

"You know, the great thing about having a Jewish best friend is that I know you'll be here on Sunday morning," I said. *Just keep pretending.*

Ariela smiled at me. I opened the screen door and brushed past her. Her smile faded.

"Hi, Mr. and Mrs. Spieler," I said to Ariela's parents, who were relaxing in t-shirts and jeans on the couch, cups of coffee next to them and pieces of the *Arizona Republic* in their laps.

Mr. Spieler waved without looking up. Mrs. Spieler looked up. "Hi, Medley. This is a lovely surprise. How are you?"

"My mom had an emergency. She and Dad are at the hospital."

"Oh my goodness, Medley. What happened?" she said.

Ariela hurried over and stood before me. Mr. Spieler looked up from his paper, concern etched on his face.

"When I woke up a few minutes ago she was on the floor of the dining room. She and Dad left in an ambulance." *Breathe.*

I looked at Ariela before letting my eyes drop to the floor. She wrapped me in a big hug. I tried to squeeze the tears back, but a few dropped, catching Ariela's black tee on the shoulders.

"Do you know which hospital she's at? Would you like us to take you there?" Mrs. Spieler asked.

"I don't know which hospital. Probably Desert Hospital,

since it's close." My voice caught, and I inhaled as steadily as I could. "Dad told me to text him if I needed anything."

Mrs. Spieler walked toward me and wrapped me in a warm hug, the sort my mom gave me when I was little. I sank into her, taking in the soft scent of her perfume. Ariela had told me once that it was called Wings, and we'd sprayed ourselves with it a couple of times when we were younger, pretending we were angels.

"Oh, dear Medley," she said.

I remembered when she'd hugged me like this last—it was right before Nana's funeral.

After a few moments, Ariela tapped me on the shoulder. I looked up. She had a glass of dark bubbly soda in a glass, no ice.

"Dr. Pepper," she said. I took the glass and swallowed a few gulps. The fizz burned in the back of my throat.

I wiped my mouth with the back of my hand. "Thanks, Ar— Aaron," I said.

"Want to hang out in my room?" she asked.

"Sure. Is that okay, Mrs. Spieler?" I asked, turning to

Ariela's mother, willing away the glassy look I felt in my eyes.

"Of course, Medley. You never even need to ask."

Mrs. Spieler looked like she was about tousle my hair, but she lowered her hand and gave a small smile instead. Ariela and I headed down the hall. She took a seat at her swiveling black desk chair, and I sat down on the green comforter of her full-sized bed.

Ariela's room looked stark and, to be frank, barren. Apart from the bed, the desk chair, and the boxy black wooden desk from IKEA, the surface of which was completely clear, there really wasn't much to it. She had a poster of Pink Floyd's "The Wall" on the wall over her bed. Otherwise the walls were covered only with taupe paint. She had a short black bookcase neatly lined with books along the short wall next to her bed. Looking around, I realized that this was how Ariela had always lived her life: with a carefully maintained appearance that no one would be able to pierce without her permission. To the unwary eye, this was the room of a tween boy. But it was so much more than that. I pulled my knees up to my chest. We sat in silence for a minute or two.

"Still got your treasure chest?" I said at last.

Ariela opened the mirrored closet door, removing several boxes from a corner of the closet before picking up a small, flat wooden chest with a combination lock. She turned the dial until the lock clicked open. Removing the lock, she opened the lid, revealing the contents within. A dozen wrapped pieces of Dubble Bubble gum were scattered on top, and underneath was a stack of thick, purple notebooks—Ariela's journals. I knew that because I'd seen her write in them here in her room, away from prying eyes. She'd read one of the entries to me once. As far as I knew, no one else had ever seen them. A new addition to the treasure box was a Pride flag, all rainbow colors, pasted to underside of the box's lid. Ariela tossed me a couple of pieces of Dubble Bubble and dug around for something else. Ariela popped a piece of gum in her mouth. I pocketed the gum and lifted the cup of soda to my mouth to take another swig. I looked out the window. Ariela had the same view I had from my room, which wasn't much of a view at all.

Ariela found what she was looking for and held it up: it was a picture of the two of us when we were five. It was our first day of Kindergarten. I had my hair in pigtails, my fingers clasping the straps of my backpack and my overalls at the same time, and I was sticking out my tongue with crossed eyes. Aaron—Ariela—had on a white polo and blue jeans, and he—she—had her hands on her cheeks with her mouth open like Macauley Caulkin in *Home Alone.*

"We're goofs," I said, shaking my head.

"Isn't it weird to think that in five years, your little sib is going to be just like us in this picture?" she said.

"If the little booger even makes it." I pulled the tie out of my hair and let my hair tumble around my shoulders and face. I leaned forward, concealed by my partial cloak.

My pocket buzzed, and I reached into my pocket for my flip-phone.

"Sit tight. Emergency c-section was successful. Baby's in intensive care," the text read.

I showed Ariela the text. She looked up, her eyes full of alarm.

My heart began to thump in my chest. I shook my head. "He didn't even tell me what the baby is."

"Pretty good chance it's human," she offered.

"I meant the sex."

Ariela's eyes flashed, but she said nothing.

"Not that it matters," I said quickly.

Ariela was quiet for a moment, and then offered me her left pinky. I curled my right pinky around hers. We both hated saying sorry.

"Wanna go for a walk?" she said.

"Yeah."

"Oh, shoot. I have softball today," I muttered as we walked down the hall. "Do you think your mom would be able to take me?"

"Take you where, honey?" Mrs. Spieler said, peeking her head around the corner.

"I have a softball game this afternoon. Mom normally drives me. It's at Kiwanis. I'd walk or take my bike, but I have to bring all my gear with me, and the bus only runs once an hour, so...."

"I'm sorry, Medley—Aaron's Dad and I have a charity dinner to set up for at the *shul*. We're going to be gone from about one o'clock on."

"Oh." I looked at my phone. "Actually, I have a friend whose parents might be able to pick me up. Thanks anyway, Mrs. S."

I texted Tiffany and stuck my phone in my back pocket.

"Where are you guys headed?" Ariela's mom asked.

"Just around the neighborhood," Ariela said.

"Okay, but if it gets hot, you need to come back in."

"Okay, Mom," Ariela said. We filled a couple water bottles with filtered water from the Spielers' fridge and walked outside.

"Where should we go?" I asked as we paused at the end of the walkway in front of her house. I avoided making eye-contact with her.

"Wanna grab our bikes and go for a ride?"

I nodded, so she grabbed her blue mountain bike and black helmet from her garage and walked it back to my house where I got my purple cruiser and matching helmet. Ariela gestured toward the silver sparkling streamers on my handles and said, "Where'd you get those?"

I snapped my helmet in place. "Target. Want to go there?"

Ariela eyed her mountain bike. "I don't think those would really go with my bike."

The left side of my mouth curled up as I ran the streamers on the left handle through my fingers. "We could trade," I said.

"Really?"

I unsnapped my helmet. "You can borrow the helmet, too. But if you give me lice and I have to shave my head...."

"Don't worry, I'd never mess with those lovely locks," Ariela said, grinning back.

We switched bikes and put our bottles of water in the bottle holders. I pushed off and began to pedal. The tread on Ariela's tires created noticeably more resistance than my tires.

I yelled behind me, "You really ought to consider getting a cruiser. They don't take nearly as much effort to ride."

"I have to keep my legs manly and buff, don't you know?" Ariela shouted back.

I snorted. *Silly boy. Girl.*

"So where are we headed?" I said once Ariela had caught up to me and was pedaling easily beside me.

"Hey, we've got all morning and early afternoon. Want to go to Tempe Town Lake?

"And do what? Go to the café at TCA and eat overpriced food?"

Ariela ignored that. "We could go to the art gallery and pretend to be Parisian art critics," she said. "Or we could hang out outside next to the infinity pool near the fireplace and act like we're celebrities."

I shook my head as I leaned into a right turn, heading north toward our school. "Meh. Hoity toity isn't going to do it for me today. Besides, that's practically Scottsdale. I think I'd rather stay close, especially if I have to get myself to softball on my own. Want to go to Gold Brew instead?"

"Sure," Ariela said.

We both circled around to head south toward Gold Brew, a locally owned coffee shop on the northeast corner of Southern and McClintock, less than a mile from where we lived. We locked our bikes up at the bike rack next to the front door and walked in. Stained-glass windows from defunct churches stood perched against the clear windows. Dark polished wood lined the front counter, and a glass pastry case stood to the right of the register. A tall, slim blond woman, old enough to be a college student, smiled at us as we approached.

"What can I get for you?" she asked.

I dug in my pockets. A crumpled five-dollar bill emerged in my hand. I set the bill on the counter.

"Could I have a tall latte in a mug, please?" I asked.

"Sure thing," she said, and rang me up.

"You brought money, right?" I said, turning to Ariela.

"Of course. You never know when you're going to need money for a buzz."

"Oh my god, dude. We're not druggies."

The blond barista glanced up from the register, her eyes moving swiftly from me to Ariela. She said nothing as she handed me my change. I dropped it in the tip jar as heat rose from my neck. I drew my right hand over my eyes. Ariela smirked.

"What would you like?" the barista asked Ariela.

"Same thing, but could I have a sprinkle of cinnamon on top?" Ariela said.

"Oh, me, too, please," I said quickly.

Our barista smiled. "You got it."

She took Ariela's money, made change, and turned to make the drinks. Ariela laughed at me. *No way to be invisible if you're a brown-skinned female athlete—not in a place as white as Tempe,* I thought. I shook my head and looked around for a table. All the ones up front were taken, so I led Ariela to the back corner, a dimly lit area where stacks of games were piled onto a tall bookshelf on one wall. A gleaming pine two-person table with matching wooden chairs was free. I sat and turned on the miniature lamp on the table, which cast a warm glow on the table and our faces. Once the barista called out our drinks, I grabbed the thick brown coffee mugs from the counter and brought them back to our table, setting one in front of Ariela and wrapping my hands around the other one. We both sipped. My phone began to ring. It was Dad.

"Hang on, it's my dad," I said. I answered the call as I got up to walk outside.

"Hey, Dad," I said. "How's Mom?"

"She's recovering," he said in a low voice. I heard a click in the background, and then he spoke again in a regular voice. "She's sleeping right now."

"How's the baby?"

There was a pause before he began. "You have a baby brother, Medley."

A brother.

"And he's okay? What's his name?"

"Mark Patrick."

"He's in the NICU still?"

I heard a sigh. "Yes. He's in critical condition. His lungs aren't fully developed, so he's having trouble breathing."

"Wow." I gripped the phone. "Wow."

I have a brother.

"Yeah." We both paused. "Listen, Medley, I don't think your mom and I will be able to come back today. You should probably call your coach and let her know you can't go to your softball game."

"Do you want me to go to the hospital?"

"No. There's not much to do here. Can you take care of yourself while we're gone?"

"Sure, Dad."

"Okay. Just so you know, there's some emergency money inside my red socks in the back of my sock drawer, so go ahead and order yourself a pizza or something."

I kept my evening plans to myself.

"Thanks, Dad."

"Love you, Medley-girl."

Tears stung my eyes.

"Love you, too. Bye."

"Bye."

I put my phone in my back pocket as I opened the front door of the coffee shop. A rush of air, cooler than the warm spring air outside, greeted me. I slid into my seat and wiped away tears from my face.

"What's up?" Ariela asked, but when I looked at her she was looking over my head as she sipped her coffee. I looked up to see who she was talking to.

"Yeah, what's up you guys?"

And there was Cynthia, shadowed by one of her blond cronies with braces and a single large pimple on her chin, poorly covered by foundation and powder. The blemished girl glanced at me and then looked away with disdain. Cynthia, meanwhile, was making moony eyes at Ariela. If I'd been drinking my latte then, I would have choked on it. I held my breath, distracted and wide-eyed at the scene before me. Ariela set down her coffee mug and maintained eye contact with Cynthia—probably to avoid looking at me.

"Hi, Cynthia. Hi, Melinda," Ariela said.

I shot Ariela a look. How did she know Blemished Blond's name when I didn't?

Cynthia pulled an empty chair from another table and sat down next to us, setting a chilled bottle of water next to her. Melinda hovered behind her. "I heard about what you did at the sock hop. That was pretty bad-ass of you to stand up to Brantley."

"Thank you," Ariela said.

Cynthia set her elbows on the table and propped her chin on her hands, millimeters from where Ariela's hands rested around her mug. "I was wondering if you were planning to come to the Hummingbirds game tonight. It would be great to see you."

My jaw fell. Ariela grinned at Cynthia.

"Sure. I love rooting for the ladies."

"Great!" she said, flashing Ariela a blindingly bright smile. "I'll see you this afternoon then."

Her hand brushed Ariela's as she got up. She wiggled her fingers goodbye as she left. I watched her till she was all the way out the door, and then I turned back to Ariela.

"For a minute there, I forgot you were a girl," I said in a low voice. I slurped foam off the top of my drink.

"Hey, who says girls can't like girls?" she said.

I looked up. "What?"

"I'm serious," she said. She sipped her latte.

I pushed my mug several inches in front of me and folded my arms. "Supposing for a moment you're interested in girls as a trans-girl," I said, my voice even lower than it was before, "Cynthia? Really?!"

"She's cute," she said, swirling the wooden stirrer in her

mug.

I stared at my friend, wondering if she'd lost her mind.

"She's a great ball player, too."

I stared at Ariela. She stared back.

I broke the silence. "Well, no way am I missing this softball game. Can't wait to see this pan out." *Especially when she finds out that you're not who she thinks you are.*

Ariela shrugged. I sighed.

We sat silently together for several minutes, and my mind wandered as I stared out the stained-glass window at the warped images beyond. The precarious thread by which my new brother's life was hanging came rushing back to me. I set down my mug and put my head in my hands. The dam broke, and tears streamed down my face and fell to the table.

"You want to talk about it?" Ariela asked quietly.

I shook my head, dragging in a deep breath. A long minute stretched out in silence between us, and then I used my hands to wipe the tears away.

"It's got to be really hard to be dealing with something this scary happening in your family," Ariela said.

She waited. I took a deep breath. This is what we did whenever one of us was upset. The other one gave the one who was upset a chance to gather their thoughts, organize them, and get them out—not necessarily in that order.

"I can't believe what's happening with Mark. I didn't even know how I felt about him at first, but now that he's in the world, I want him to keep being in it. without Mom and Dad there with me—with them at the hospital—" I struggled to put the words together.

I paused, searching for the words that would clarify.

Ariela's eyes filled a bit, and she locked onto my gaze.

We sat in quiet while one minute stretched into another. Once again I wondered who I was and where I had come from. I still knew next to nothing about my biological roots. So maybe my mom hadn't wanted me, and maybe she hid me from my father. But I bet my grandparents would have wanted me. Right? *Or maybe they were self-righteous jerks who disowned my mom when they found out she was pregnant out of wedlock.*

I didn't know how things had gone down with my bio-mom, my bio-grandparents, or my bio-dad. I knew nothing about my biological family. There wasn't much my parents needed to worry about in my case, at least not yet, since I didn't have much interest in dating, much less anything more serious. But what if it were me? Would they force me to give up my baby? Would they throw me out of the house for shaming them?

They could. That thought echoed coldly in my brain.

I looked at Ariela. She looked back at me. Between us, the same question echoed silently: "Who am I?"

Chapter 6

Strike two!" the umpire called. My hair swayed behind me. I set my stance again and waited for the pitcher to wind up.

Out of the park, Medley. For Mark. And Mom.

I swung.

I missed.

The Hummingbirds' second loss of the season ended on my strikeout, leaving the team with a record of 3-2.

"At least you struck out swinging, right?" Ariela said with a half-grin as I packed my gear in the dugout. Heat rose up my neck. I shook my head.

After the requisite shuttle runs and post-game lecture on how we could have improved, Cynthia stood at the other end of the dugout listening to two of her minions talk about how great she did. "Well, it doesn't make much difference how great I am if I'm teammates with people who don't know how to compete," she said.

I jerked my head in Cynthia's direction and found her side-eyeing me. I could hear Coach Marge talking to the other team's coach by first base; she hadn't heard. I zipped my bag closed with force and was about to head out with Ariela when I realized Ariela was no longer there. Suddenly Cynthia's voice was crooning. My skin crawled.

"Aaron, it's so great having you out there rooting for us. Thanks so much for your support. It means so much to have great fans out in the stands," Cynthia said.

Stealing another glance, I could see that Cynthia was practically hanging all over Ariela, and "Aaron" was eating up the attention. I grabbed my bag and stomped out.

"Medley, wait up!" Tiffany called.

Tiffany's parents had agreed to pick me up so I could get to the game without riding the bus. I had told them nothing of my day so far—just that my parents weren't available to take me. *Amazing that Ariela showed up after all that, given that she had no ride, either.* Tiffany's family were probably wondering where I was going. I kept my pace steady and continued walking away from the softball fields. Hastening footsteps grew louder behind me, and then Tiffany was next to me.

"Hey, girl, where you going? Don't you want a ride home?"

I stiffened my chin and walking. "I think I'll take the bus."

Tiffany kept stride with me as I walked past the outfield fence and onto the sidewalk that would eventually lead out of the park. When she spoke again, her voice was softer. "Hey, I know that was a rough way to end the game. It could have happened to any of us."

"It happened to me," I snapped.

Tiffany flinched.

Tears began to well up in my eyes. I walked faster.

"You just seem... not very much yourself. Since before the game even started. Look, I get it if you don't want to talk, but if you ever do, you can always talk to me, okay?"

With a burst of movement she got in front of me and turned, blocking my path.

"Okay?" she said again.

I folded my arms and looked at the ground. In my periphery I saw her move, and I looked up. She peered at me, waiting. I gave the OK sign with my left hand. She opened her arms. I stepped in and buried my face in her shoulder. She squeezed me tight, till the trembling stopped and my breathing returned to normal. She looked at me and our eyes locked. There was strength in her look. She spoke her support without a single word.

Then she stepped aside and I resumed my pace. I didn't look back. If I had, I might have seen her staring after me. If I had, she might have seen hot tears streaming down my face.

By the time I got home, it was nearly eight and already dark. As I walked in, the warm glow of light from Ariela's house made familiar items visible. Shadows lurked everywhere. I checked my phone, which hadn't rung once since I walked off the softball field. It was dead. *Oh.* I plugged it in at my desk, flopped onto my bed, and reached over to press the on button a few minutes later. The voicemail notification popped up. I dialed my voicemail and listened. "You have three messages," the voice said.

As I listened, I heard my dad's increasingly frantic voice letting me know he was still with Mom and the baby and wanting to know where I was. I called him back right away.

"Medley, where have you been?" Dad hissed in a loud whisper. I heard the sound of a door click shut in the background.

"I've been at softball. I just got home."

"You went to softball? Are you kidding me right now?" He wasn't whispering. I held the phone away from my ear.

"What else was I supposed to do? You're not here, and you don't want me there, so—"

"Don't start giving me crap, Medley. I have enough to worry about here without wondering where you are. It's selfish of you to run off without any way for me to reach you. Besides, I asked you to stay home."

I held my breath.

"Are you there?"

I hiccuped and winced. "I'm sorry."

Breathe. Slowly.

When he spoke again, Dad's voice was softer. "I'm sorry,

too, Medley-girl. It's hard on all of us, and I know you're there alone. I was calling to tell you that there have been complications with your brother, and I need to stay overnight. I need you to keep your phone charged and your ringer on in case anything changes. I wish I could be there with you."

"Okay," I said.

He sighed. "You know Mom and I love you, right?"

I held my breath and squeezed my eyes shut. "Yes."

His voice broke. "Talk soon. And hang in there, Medley-girl."

"Bye."

I clicked the red button to disconnect. Then I stared at my phone, numb.

My brother. My mother. My father. Ariela. Cynthia. Tiffany. Lost the game. You lost the game. You're a loser.

I plugged in my phone again and turned the ringer volume up. Then I put my head under the pillow so no one could hear me.

The next morning I woke up early, before my usual

alarm. I wasn't hungry, so as soon as I was ready I was out the door and on my way, triple-checking that my phone was tucked into my back pocket. I didn't stop by Ariela's house. At the end of the street where I made my first turn, I thought I heard someone call my name, so I began to jog. I thought I heard my name again; this time I broke into a run. Then my run became a sprint, and I ran as hard as I could until I couldn't hear anything anymore except my own heartbeat pulsing like cannon-fire. I didn't slow down until I was a block from school. Then I walked, breathing deeply and wiping sweat from my forehead. My phone rang then, and I checked it. "Aaron," the name read. I ignored the call and used the opportunity to text Dad and let him know I was at school and that I'd have my phone on vibrate if he needed me during the day. My phone rang again as I was about to hit send, and I accidentally answered the call—also from Ariela. I hung up and kept walking. I couldn't face someone who knew me as well as she did, not even by phone. She'd hear it all before I got two words out and I'd unravel.

I crossed the threshold into the building and shuffled

toward homeroom, my backpack hanging low off one shoulder.

"Hey, Ms. Medley," Ms. Feliz called.

I turned to see her hurrying toward me, dressed in a flowy silk shirt and shiny black leggings. Her hair was pulled up in a French twist and she had two pencils sticking out of her hair. She looked like an artist. "How's your April piece coming along?"

Ms. Feliz's eyebrows furrowed as she watched my face fall.

"Not done yet, eh?" she asked.

I shook my head.

"No worries. You coming to newspaper staff tomorrow after school?"

"I don't know. My mom just had my baby brother and he's in intensive care. Dad's at the hospital, too, and I think he wants me to be home as much as possible. I'm not sure."

"Oh, Medley, I'm so sorry."

I stood silently and looked at a chip in the floor tile.

"Listen, how about if you head to the office and let the secretary know you're there to see Ms. Hopley. Have you talked to Ms. Hopley before?"

I shook my head.

"She's one of our school counselors. She may be able to help you talk through some things and figure out a plan."

I looked up. "What kind of plan?"

Ms. Feliz smiled gently. "Whatever kind of plan you need to move forward with everything that's changing around you."

I looked behind me toward my homeroom class, where I saw Tiffany just walking in. She waved, her eyes full of curiosity and concern. I waved back and returned my gaze to Ms. Feliz.

"What about homeroom?"

"I'll let your homeroom teacher know what's happening. Is it Mr. Irwin?"

I nodded.

"Okay. You want me to walk you to the office?"

I was about to shake my head no, but then I saw Ariela, and she saw me.

"Sure," I said, allowing my hair to cascade in front of me as I followed Ms. Feliz, watching her low black leather boots click across the tiled floor.

"Medley," Ariela said, as I passed by. I shook my head and kept walking. She wouldn't come after me this time. And this time a feeling of dread and sadness fell over me like a lead blanket. I felt so heavy I could barely walk, but I kept shuffling forward. *Everything you do makes it worse, Medley. You make every single thing worse.*

I plopped into one of the orange plastic chairs in the main office while Ms. Feliz moved down the inner hallway to Ms. Hopley's office. I waited, feeling the eyes of the school secretary on me. Soon Ms. Hopley emerged with Ms. Feliz. Ms. Feliz gave me an encouraging smile and walked out. I watched her walk out before returning my attention to Ms. Hopley. She was a short, older woman, probably nearing sixty, with salt and pepper curly hair, glasses, and an average frame. She smelled like sweet incense. When I stood, I found I was half a head taller than she was. A half-smile involuntarily crossed my lips, and Ms. Hopley met it with a full smile of her own.

"I'm Ms. Hopley, and you're Medley," she said. It was a statement, not a question.

I nodded.

"Are you up for a visit in my office for a few minutes?" she asked.

I shrugged.

"Well, I'll lead the way, and if you want to join me, just follow along. Otherwise you can sit back down on that super-comfy chair for a while." She winked before she turned.

I shook my head. Ms. Hopley was weird, but she seemed all right.

Her office made me pause. The wall opposite the windows was royal purple, but the remaining walls were a lighter, matted lavender. Whatever scent clung to her was stronger in this room. Unlike the office, there was a plush cloth chair that reclined. Ms. Hopley gestured for me to take a seat there. I sank into it.

"Do they know you have this chair in here?" I asked.

"Sure. I bought it. And I like to sit in it when I don't need to be at my computer."

She smiled. I shifted in my seat, aware of being the center of her attention and wondering what she'd be doing if she weren't meeting with a student or working at her computer.

Silence lengthened between us like Pinocchio's nose, but I didn't detect a lie between us. I felt like a stained glass window in her presence.

"Is there anything you'd like to talk about, Medley?"

I shook my head and studied my hands.

"That's all right. Sometimes a bit of quiet is preferable to chatter, isn't it?"

Light glinted in her eyes as I looked up. She turned her chair and looked out the window. I followed her gaze. A hummingbird flew high and dive-bombed.

"It's guarding its territory," Ms. Hopley said. I stood and moved closer to watch it dive and hover.

"Hummingbirds are known for their ability to flap their wings rapidly, and sometimes they're known for their beauty, but what many folks don't necessarily know is that they're fiercely possessive. They don't want anyone messing with what's theirs." Ms. Hopley said, still watching the hummingbird.

She and I stared out the window for a while, till the hummingbird disappeared above the tree.

"It's nice in here. It's like an oasis in the middle of all this school-ness," I said, gesturing toward her door.

"Thank you. I spend quite a lot of time in here, so I wanted to make it into a space that reflects me."

"I dig it. My best friend's room isn't like that at all. His room is so bare."

"Not everyone wants to be seen. It takes vulnerability to let someone else in on a space that reflects you."

"Yeah. I get that, too." I thought about telling her about my password-protected journal on my computer at home, but I didn't. I caught sight of the clock on Ms. Hopley's wall. Just then, the warning bell for first period rang. I hadn't heard the bell signifying the start of homeroom. I stood.

"Time for class. If you want to stop by again during your study hall or before or after school, you know where to find me." Ms. Hopley stood and opened the door for me.

I pulled on my backpack and lifted my hand in a wave before walking out. As I walked to class, visions of hummingbirds and purple hues and deep brown eyes filled my mind.

Monday, April 4, 2016

It's been less than two weeks since I last wrote, but it feels like two centuries.

1) Mom had the baby prematurely. I woke up and found her bleeding all over the floor yesterday before paramedics came to take her to the hospital.

2) The baby is a boy. Or has a penis, at least. His name is Mark Patrick. He's in the Neonatal Intensive Care Unit (NICU). They've got nurses and doctors there all the time to monitor him. His lungs are all messed up, apparently. This happens with premature babies. He's not a super-preemie. He was born at 33 weeks. But that's four weeks earlier than "full-term," according to the baby book Mom was reading.

3) Dad didn't want me to go with them, but he didn't want me going anywhere else, either, so I was supposed to miss my softball game last night. I went anyway. After I had the game-losing strikeout of the softball game, I got home and got yelled at by Dad for not being available on the phone that they never wanted to give me in the first place. OH, and:

4) Ariela told me while we were at Gold Brew yesterday that she thinks she has a thing for girls. Cynthia in particular (who completely swooned over him yesterday, also at Gold Brew, AND at the game. Stalker, much?).

5) I avoided Ariela on the way to school this morning. When I got there, Ms. Feliz asked me how my April piece was coming. I haven't done a thing on it. She asked if I'd be staying for newspaper tomorrow, and I told her about Mark. She took me to see one of the school counselors, Ms. Hopley.

6) Ms. Hopley is nice. Weird. In a good way, I think. Her office doesn't even feel like an office. It's like... I don't know. A meditation room? We barely talked. And when we did talk, it was about the hummingbird zooming around outside her window. She told me hummingbirds are "fiercely possessive."

I don't know if I'm possessive. I'm pretty chill, mostly. But I'm a mess right now. I mean, I don't care who (whom?) my other friends hang out with. Unless my best friend is romantically interested in my nemesis. Gees, Ariela, really?

Also, how does that even work? People think you're a boy your whole life, and then you tell your female bestie you're

a girl, and then you tell her you're interested in girls? I mean...
wouldn't it be easier just to be a boy who likes girls?

And then I realize I'm a total jerk, because Ariela isn't
randomly saying she's a she. She is a she, even though she looks
like a boy. And there are plenty of people who go by the
pronoun "she" who also like girls.

Except that Cynthia doesn't have a clue. And Ariela's a
fool if she tells Cynthia anything that she doesn't want the
whole school to know.

Why's everything so complicated all of a sudden?

I felt powerless yesterday after the game and after
talking to Dad, and then this morning when I couldn't even
face Ariela. I don't think I've ever felt as lost as I did then.

Tiffany followed me as I left the game last night. She
stopped me, and then she gave me a hug. I cried in her arms.
All this emotional crap came out of me wordlessly and I was
shaking. Then she looked at me like I was the only person in
the entire universe in that moment, and I felt... I don't know.
Centered? I ended up walking away, but it felt like she
imparted a bit of herself in that look.

Here, writing here, I feel more like myself again.

No one can take my words away from me.

Chapter 7

That night, car-beams bounced off my bedroom wall. I heard the garage door open and I hurried out of my room and down the hall. My dad opened the door from the garage, and the sour smell of overworn clothes drifted into the room. He shut the door behind him. His eyes were red.

"I'll be right back, okay, Medley? Then we can talk." He trudged past me to his room and shut the door. Soon I heard water streaming.

A few minutes later, the water fell silent. I sat at the dining room table, waiting silently. When he came out, Dad had on a clean t-shirt and jeans and smelled like soap. He sat down next to me and rubbed his jaw.

"Your brother is going to be in the NICU for another few weeks."

A few weeks?

"I'm going back to stay with your mother again tonight at the hospital, and tomorrow or Wednesday she should be released to go home. After that, we'll bring you with us to the NICU to meet your brother. I brought some money for you so you can buy food. This probably means ordering takeout pizza for dinner the next day or two, but you're old enough to take care of yourself now." Dad rubbed his neck with one hand. Then he rubbed his eyes with the other. "In the meantime, I'm going to pack some extra clothes for me, your mom, and the baby."

"Dad?" I said.

He met my gaze. "Yes, Medley?"

"You haven't said his name."

"What?"

"You haven't said his name since you told me what it was yesterday morning. You keep calling him 'the baby.'"

Dad's eyes were wells flowing with raw emotion. Resignation seeped into them. He blinked.

He got up without a word and went to his room to begin packing. By the time he emerged, he had everything he needed packed up in one large suitcase. I sat in my chair, motionless. I didn't look up when he gave me a kiss on the forehead and put five twenties in front of me.

"We all need to do everything we can to hold ourselves together right now. Can I count on you, slugger?"

I nodded, thinking of all the times Dad had given me a pep-talk before a Little League game.

"Dad, is it okay if I go to newspaper staff after school tomorrow? I have a story due that I've barely started, and it's got to be done tomorrow if I want it to go in the paper."

"As long as your phone is charged and you have it with you, that's fine. But then you need to come straight home, okay?"

"Thanks, Dad."

I got up to give him a hug. He gave me a quick half-hug and a pat on the back with one hand, his other hand still holding on to the rolling suitcase.

"Gotta get going. See you soon. Love you, Medley-girl."

The door to the garage clicked shut behind him.

"Bye, Dad."

I looked around. It felt cold and vacant. I walked past the living room and exited onto the patio, where the open sky glittered with stars and a warm breeze fragrant with jasmine blossoms tickled my skin.

"Hey," a voice said.

I looked over and spotted Ariela peeking around the bamboo.

"Hey," I said.

Ariela easily jumped over the wall and came over to stand beside me. We looked up at the night sky.

"It's nice out tonight, huh?"

"It is," I murmured. I crossed my arms and looked back at the sky, searching for familiar constellations.

We stood there for a while without speaking, allowing silence to do her slow chore of mending. Then, without turning my gaze, I reached out my pinkie, and I felt Ariela's pinkie wrap around mine.

"You really like Cynthia a lot." It was more of a comment than a question.

"She really likes me. And I like being liked, not gonna lie."

I said nothing.

"When so many people out there are so ready to hate me just because of how I identify, it's hard not to latch onto someone who clearly thinks the world of me. Know what I mean?" Ariela looked over at me.

The sarcasm on my tongue dissolved. "I just worry that she might turn out to be one of the haters once she finds out about you. I mean, she acts like such a jerk in so many other ways," I said.

Ariela shook her head. "I don't know. I mean, I know you don't like her and she hasn't gone out of her way to be nice to you, but I think there's more to her than what you see."

More silence settled between us.

"I want you to be happy," I said.

"I know. Thank you. You've always been a great friend, Medley. I appreciate you more than you know."

A shooting star flashed in the sky. As I watched, my vision seemed to shift. Hundreds of glittering stars filled the sky, and trillions more stretched beyond the reach of my sight. I felt them all.

"Are you going to newspaper staff tomorrow?" Ariela

asked, breaking the spell.

"Yeah. I got the okay from my dad to go, and then I have to come right home."

"How are things going with your mom and your brother?"

"They're okay. Mom is supposed to be released tomorrow or the next day, but Mark's not going to be released for a while."

"Sounds like jail."

"I know, right?" I paused. "I wonder if my parents are going to be able to afford whatever it costs for Mark to stay in the hospital."

Ariela and I exchanged looks. And then she reached over and enveloped me in a hug.

"It'll be okay, whatever happens. It's got to be okay," she whispered.

"I don't know, though," I said. "What if he gets worse?"

I trembled, considering the possibilities the immediate future held. Ariela rocked me gently.

"Aaron, where are you?" Ariela's mom called from inside

the house.

"I'm here at Medley's," Ariela called back, letting me go.

"It's time for dinner, bub."

Ariela squeezed my hands. "Want to come over?"

"To dinner? Don't I have to be ritually pure to eat at your house?"

Ariela chuckled. "My dear *goya*, allow me to enlighten you. Tonight you shall dine in the House of Ariela and learn all about the holy *chag* of Israel, *Pesach*. You need a lesson in Jewish traditions for your piece in the school newspaper, so dinner at my house is the perfect idea. The only question is, are you going to beat me there?"

Ariela turned for the wall, but as she moved down the wall to where the bamboo plant ended, I took the shortest route to the wall, pulled myself up on top of it, and shimmied through the bamboo. I was at her patio door a full two steps ahead of her.

"You cheated!"

"I used my ingenuity."

"Is that Medley I hear?" Ariela's dad said, coming to the

door as he wiped his hands with a handtowel. He wore an apron that said "Kiss the Kosh."

"I invited Medley over for dinner. She's worried about being ritually pure."

"Well, you already sacrificed a pair of turtledoves for your transgressions, right?" her dad asked.

I gaped at him. And then Ariela snorted, and so did her dad. I blushed, grateful once again for that blessedly dark pigment from my bio-parents' gene pool.

That evening, I had a kosher dinner for the first time in a long time. It was preceded and followed by Hebrew prayers. I closed my eyes as I listened to Ariela's mom and dad take turns chanting. How sublime, to offer words in such an intentional, grateful way all through one's meal.

"I bet this is what it was like in the early house churches of Christianity," I mused, biting into a matzo ball from my soup bowl.

"How do you mean, Medley?" Ariela's mom asked.

"From what I've read, the early Christians met in houses and prayed and ate together. The spaces weren't separate from where people normally spent time. It's different now."

"That's an interesting observation. Christianity does seem, in some quarters, to be oriented toward what happens in spaces set apart, like churches. In the Jewish world, however, or at least in the orthodox Jewish world, faith begins and ends at home. Activities at the *shul* or synagogue are an extension of that, not the other way around."

Goosebumps sailed across my arms as I considered home as the meeting-place of divine encounter. Visions of the stars from the night sky filled my imagination. The moon was there, too, full with the love of my parents. Was my bio-mom a stargazer, too? As I considered the moon, the brown eyes of an amazing softball player filled my mind's eye, and the goosebumps rippled again.

The next day, armed with info about *Pesach* and bleary-eyed from the many rabbit holes I jumped into, I considered sacred space, Jewish identity, and the rite of Passover.

The smell of glue permeated the halls. Thoughts of my parents and little brother edged into my consciousness, but there was nothing I could do about any of that except keep my phone charged and the ringer audible. Ms. Heger commented in first period that I seemed quieter than usual. By the time I got to newspaper staff after school, I was both tired and eager to get to work. Ms. Feliz looked over as I walked in.

"Ms. Blunt, you remind me of a ruby-throated hummingbird rattling the wind with her wings."

I looked down at my flowing silk top with spatters of colors all over and my tie-dyed jeggings. I shrugged. "I'm an artist."

Ms. Feliz burst out laughing. As she recovered, she walked toward me, placed a hand on each of my shoulders, looked me in the eye, and said, "You are an artist."

I tried on the role of artist as I sat down at the school computer to work on my piece for the newspaper. Not a visual artist, *per se*, but an artist who loves weaving words to describe the visual. An artist of words. A writer.

The following emerged as I sat at the computer:

You may know that Pesach, *which is the Hebrew word for 'Passover,' is coming up later this month beginning on April 22. Christians may associate* Pesach/*Passover with their own celebration of Easter. But did you know that* Pesach *is an eight-day celebration for Jewish people?*

The commemoration of Pesach *(pronounced PAY-sock) is mandated in* Torah, *the first five books of the Hebrew Bible (also known as the Old Testament by Christians), in the book of* Shemmot *or* Exodus. *The mandate is given after the story of the first passing over, which went something like this: the Pharaoh of Egypt had enslaved the Hebrew people to build his kingdom, and Moses, under divine orders, told Pharaoh to let his people go. When Pharaoh resisted, Moses warned him that plagues would come upon Egypt for his rebellion and stubbornness, but the Pharaoh was obstinate, so the plagues came. The final plague was the worst of all, in which HaShem (God himself) would pass over the homes of his people, whose doors were to be marked with the blood of a lamb, to find the homes of the Egyptians and kill their firstborn children. When*

Pharaoh's own son died in this final, terrible plague, he let Moses' people go, and they crossed out of Egypt through the Sea of Reeds (often mistakenly translated as the "Red Sea") into freedom.

When Jewish people celebrate Pesach, they are celebrating their journey to liberation. Their Pesach seder (a ritual meal) includes matzah, unleavened bread (to signify that there was no time to let leaven sit and grow as they were making their exodus out of Egypt); bitter herbs (for their loss and what they endured before freedom and on their way to freedom), something sweet (to signify the sweetness of the land of milk and honey that HaShem promised them), and the shankbone of a lamb (to signify the blood of the lamb that marked them as HaShem's own people).

Once Pesach arrives, you can try out a Pesach greeting with your Jewish friends: Chag Pesach Hameach (HOG PAY-sock ha-MAY-ock).

I stopped typing and checked the word count. It was just shy of 350 words. *Oy gevalt.*

"It's a tad long," Ms. Feliz remarked. She leaned over to scan what I'd written. "Maybe take out the references to Christianity and put in only the three most important symbols from the *seder*? And see if you can tighten up the background paragraph."

"Sure," I responded. For the next few minutes I reworked the piece until it was a hundred words shorter. I had Ms. Feliz read it over my shoulder again.

Pesach (pronounced PAY-sock) is mandated in Torah, the first five books of the Hebrew Bible. The mandate is given after the story of the first "passing over," which went something like this: the Pharoah of Egypt had enslaved the Hebrew people to build his kingdom, and Moses, under divine orders, told Pharaoh to let his people go. When Pharaoh resisted, Moses warned him that plagues would come upon Egypt for his rebellion and stubbornness. The final plague was the worst of all, in which HaShem would pass over the homes of his people, whose doors were to be marked with the blood of a lamb, to find the homes of the

Egyptians and kill their firstborn children. When Pharaoh's own son died, he let Moses' people go, and they crossed out of Egypt into freedom.

When Jewish people celebrate Pesach, *they are celebrating their journey to liberation. Their* Pesach seder *includes elements like* matzah, *i.e. unleavened bread (because there was no time to let leaven sit and grow as they were journeying to freedom); bitter herbs (for what they endured before and on their way to freedom),* and *something sweet (to signify the sweetness of the land of milk and honey that* HaShem *promised them).*

You can try out a Pesach *greeting this year with your Jewish friends:* Chag Pesach Hameach *(hog PAY-sock ha-MAY-ock)!*

"That's great, Medley, for a couple reasons. One, it's the right length. Two, it takes out references to Christianity, which strengthens its focus on Judaism. Not everything has to refer back to what you think most people will 'get,'" she said, gesturing quotation marks with her fingers. "Judaism can stand on its own two feet. It's been doing that for over five thousand years."

"That makes sense," I said, turning my gaze from her to my draft. "I like that. Judaism doesn't need to refer to anything but itself."

"I think you're onto something, Ms. Blunt," she said, grinning. "Can you think of another example in which that's the case?"

I tapped my chin with my fingers. "I saw something last spring when I was out practicing swings on the ballfield with my mom. There was this woman who was probably in her twenties—it was clear that she had spent a lot of time on her outfit and hair and stuff, and she was there with some buff guy who had a batting tee. They were on the next diamond over and she hit the ball a couple times. Her form was pretty amateur and she only made contact once. The guy she was with laughed at her, and then she didn't hit at all the rest of the time. She didn't even try. And I wonder if she would have kept trying if she had been on her own, just hitting on her own, not trying to compare herself to that buff dude who clearly had gotten thousands of hits in before that day."

"Sounds like she ended up devaluing herself when she compared herself with the person whose experience was completely different from hers," Ms. Feliz said.

"And why would you base your evaluation of yourself on someone else?" I continued. "It makes no sense to compare an apple to an orange in order to learn about the experience of an apple."

"You've hit it right on the money, my young friend," Ms. Feliz said. She patted me on the shoulder. "Save that file for me and I'll take care of the rest. Great work, Medley."

"Thanks, Ms. Feliz."

When I was done saving the file, I waved goodbye and headed home. As I walked, I pondered what the world would look like if people focused on the intrinsic value and character of a thing, group, or person, rather than comparing that thing, group, or person to what or who it was not. I also wondered whether the intrinsic value of my life was taken into consideration by my bio-mom thirteen years ago. I punched my right palm with my left fist. There were so many unanswered questions.

Who am I?

Chapter 8

In the distance a siren sounded in the dark, and my eyes flew open. It was Tuesday night. My old teddy bear, Matilda, was on my chest of drawers. I crept out of bed and wrapped her up in my arms, smelling her old familiar scent of silky baby powder before crawling back into the warmth of my covers. Just as I closed my eyes, my phone rang.

"Hey, Dad."

"Hey, are you asleep?"

"I was just about to be."

"Everything okay there?"

"Yep. Everything okay at the hospital?"

"Yes. The good news is, Mom will be discharged late tomorrow morning, so you won't be alone at night from now on. We're going to stay at the NICU as late as they'll let us, though, so you probably won't see us until after eight tomorrow evening.

Okay?"

I doubted I had a choice. "Okay," I said finally.

"We love you so much, Medley-girl. And we know this has been hard for you. We'll see you soon."

"Okay. Bye, Dad."

"Bye, slugger."

I closed my eyes again and hugged my bear, but the sleep I had been drifting into was long gone. Frustrated, I reached blindly for a book from the stack on my night table next to the bed and grabbed my reading light from the night table drawer. I flipped the switch on my reading light and pointed the beam at the books next to me, feeling oddly like the guilt-stricken, terrified character from Edgar Allen Poe's story, "The Tell-Tale Heart."

I caught sight of Nana's old breviary, a prayer book from her childhood. I opened it carefully so as not to wrinkle or tear the delicate pages. The order in which one was supposed to read the breviary was hard to decipher, so I turned the pages until I found compline, also known as night prayer, in its own little set of pages, no flipping back and forth required. Psalm 4 spoke of lying down in peace and falling asleep at once, dwelling in the safety of God.

"Well, that's not working so far," I muttered.

Then I saw Psalm 91, and the haunting melody of a setting I knew for it wrapped around me like a warm cloak.

"He who dwells in the shelter of the most high abides in the shade of the almighty," I sang in a soft voice. God was making Godself felt in my words, the words that had crossed the lips of thousands in full voice and in whispers.

But why "he who dwells?" Why not "she who dwells?" Why is what is masculine always and everywhere defined as the norm? What if the feminine were the norm, even for a moment?

Ariela came to mind, and I imagined her praying the psalms in Hebrew while using feminine pronouns for both *HaShem* and herself, and my stomach dropped. I inhaled sharply. The whole world seemed quite still.

I crawled out of bed and hurried to the computer in Mom and Dad's library.

Tuesday, April 5, 2016

What if I didn't have to pretend like half the human race is included in religious prayer when it isn't? What if we simply were included?

Does anyone else do this? I mean, clearly not so much in western religions, but what about other religions? I know that there are goddesses in Hinduism and such. And definitely in Paganism, if Terry Pratchett's books are accurate.

I don't know. There's so much to find out.

I sat back at my chair, flustered.

I think of what Ms. Feliz was saying earlier—the mainstream lens isn't the one we always have to bow to. The voice of the minority has its own story to share without any reference whatever to the mainstream or majority. And if that's true in general, it's true for me which means my experience is valid, and the message that American culture keeps handing me—that everything superior and most holy is male, and everything feminine is lesser—is not valid according to my experience. Or maybe "not valid" isn't the way to say it—maybe "not relevant" is the way to say it.

For the sake of a thought experiment, let's say salvation weren't even a religious issue. If salvation weren't an issue, much less the issue, what would religious faith be about?

I'm curious. I've never thought of what religion would look like without salvation until just this second. And the thought that comes to mind next is, "What would be the point?"

And if I edge just a little further from the circle of my understanding of faith—and right now I'm thinking of Nana's faith—I can see that if salvation weren't an issue, people wouldn't be afraid of losing their faith, at least not because they'd think they were going to hell.

And if they weren't afraid of going to hell, then maybe they wouldn't be so attached to the dumb things religious leaders say, like the ones who backed HB2.

But if there were no salvation in the mix, what would be compelling about religion in the first place? Is there religion that doesn't involve salvation?

My body is shaking now as I consider all this. Because

*now I wonder if the only way to get beyond stupid religious
ideas is to get rid of salvation, too, and if there's no salvation,
then what is the point of faith at all?*

I blinked away stray tears and rubbed my eyes with the
back of my hand. I saved the journal file, shut down the
computer, and returned to my room to crawl into bed.

I hugged Matilda tight and buried my face in my pile
until, after what seemed like hours, I fell into a dreamless sleep.

The next day I woke up with drool on my chin and an
alarm blaring in my ear. I opened my eyes in a squint and saw
that I had exactly thirty-one minutes to get to school. *Oh, crud.*

I leaped out of bed, threw my hair up, took a shower,
scrubbed my teeth, tied my shoes as I waited for two frozen
waffles to heat up in the toaster, and ran out the door after
checking to make sure the lock was on. Ariela was waiting for
me at the end of my driveway on her bike.

"I figured you were running late, so I thought I'd meet
you, and if you didn't want to walk with me, you could run to

school again. Except this time I have a bike," she said.

I snorted. "Well, bikes it is. And yes, I'm running late. And I *guess* it's okay if you ride with me," I said.

"Did you have a hot date last night?" Ariela said.

"Totally," I said, rolling my eyes.

"Might as well, right? I'm a little envious."

Images of Ariela and Cynthia making out popped into my head and I gagged. Ariela almost fell off her bike laughing.

"Gross," I said.

When she recovered herself, she got back on her bike and we began to pedal. As we turned the first corner, she said in a raised voice, "So what kept you up last night?"

"Just thinking," I answered back.

"About?"

"Religion."

"You stayed up late thinking about religion? Seriously? You sound like a rabbi," she joked.

I didn't laugh. I pumped my legs harder, making Ariela push harder to keep up with me.

"We're going to get there in plenty of time, for the

record," she said.

"I just want to get there," I said.

A few minutes later, we arrived, winded. Cynthia was hovering by the bike rack waiting for Ariela. She ignored me.

"See ya," I said, and walked toward the main doors.

"Why do you hang out with her?" I heard Cynthia say to Ariela.

I pushed through the front doors, not waiting to hear the answer.

The day wore on slowly, and I was distracted all the while. Ms. Feliz remarked toward the end of first period, "I'm surprised you have no opinion to offer today, Ms. Blunt."

All day my mind swirled with thoughts of religion, faith, femininity, and masculinity. It was as though all the puzzle pieces had spontaneously changed shape, and I didn't know what the picture was supposed to look like anymore. When I began to work out one thing, another thing fell apart.

I considered Ariela and her deeply Jewish faith as well as her emerging gender identity. I thought of all the world religions and how convinced they all were that they were "right." If God knew us from when we were in the womb, then why did God not give Ariela the right body parts when God had a chance? Or what if Ariela *was* born with the right body parts, and she was *still* supposed to be a girl?

"What's up with you today?" Ariela said as we unlocked our bikes following the final bell.

I shook my head silently.

"You know I'm here to listen anytime you need me, right?"

But I wasn't ready to share my questions about Ariela with Ariela. "I'm worried about Mark," I said.

Ariela looked down, her face turning pink. "I'm sorry," she said.

"Don't be," I hurried to say.

"Have you heard anything?" Ariela said.

"Mom and Dad are still going to visit him regularly, but Mom should be discharged today. They're going to come home sometime after eight, which is when visiting hours end."

"You want to come over to my house while you wait?"

"Naw, that's okay. I could use some time to just think."

"Sure. Of course," she said. We pedaled toward home. I waved goodbye when she made her turn. Then I made my way to my house. When I arrived, my parents' car was in the driveway. My pulse quickened.

I pedaled hard and rode into the garage, where I ditched my bike and hurried into the house. Mom and Dad were at the kitchen table, Mom with her head in her hands. She didn't look up as I came inside. Dad looked up, met my confused eyes, and shook his head.

At a loss, I loped to my room, heat growing both in my belly and in my tear-flooded eyes. Dad came in a couple minutes later and pulled my rocking chair over to my bed, where I was curled up cross-legged under my comforter, my shoes on the floor next to me. I hugged Matilda and staring at my comforter.

"Honey," he said.

I looked up.

"Honey, I have some bad news. Things went sideways." He hiccuped and drew in a ragged breath. "They did everything they could, but they couldn't get him back."

He put his face in his hands.

Mark Patrick, my brother, my adopted brother, my parents' bio-kid, the kid who was going to replace me, the kid who had replaced me, the kid who would never replace me, was gone.

I got up, grabbed my sneakers from my bedroom floor, and ran out of the house. I ran as the sun beat down on me, my shoes still in hand, until my feet blistered, then bled. And still I ran, and ran, and ran, willing the pain in my feet and my lungs to overcome the ocean that threatened to crush me, all of me. I ran down neighborhood streets, ignored the gawkers who drove by, finally pulled on my shoes with trembling hands as I waited at the red light to cross Southern at Country Club, and then kept running, my feet aching and staining my shoes with blood, until I reached the crossover bridge at US-60. I ran across that, too, and slowed as I descended into Hudson Park. Kids shrieked from the playground, and I wasn't sure then if the burning in my lungs was from my run as much as it was from thinking of my brother who would never play on the playground, never learn to play ball, never do any of the things I learned to do.

My head was a forest fire all ablaze. A deep, throbbing

beat pulsed in the midst of it, as if a drummer was saying her farewell to her dwelling-place. I sat on the dry grass under a tall, old tree. This tree had been here before any of Tempe had been built up. It grew and it saw, and it would be here long after our memories had dimmed and vanished into the breath of new generations. It would keep standing after all that, being itself, being shade for someone who sought it.

It was warm, but I pulled my hair out of its bun and let it tumble down my shoulders and stomach. My hair reached the ground where I sat. I pushed it over my shoulders so it would rest on my back, and I leaned against the tree again. The fire ebbed, just a little, but the beat continued, pounding in my head.

I sat and watched moms and dads play with their kids and fiddle on their phones. I resented them for carrying on as if it were a normal day.

The sky began to glimmer gold and orange. It was time to go back. I wasn't sure I could face my parents' sorrow, or my own. But I began to limp back, one step at a time. I couldn't let my parents lose another one of their kids today.

Chapter 9

A nightmare chased me down night after night. In my dream, Mark was five years old, with dark skin and a full head of jet-black hair down to his waist. He tugged on my shirt to play with him. "Meeeeeed-weeeeeey!" he'd say with a lisp, and I turned away and began to run. He ran after me, but I ran faster. He kept running after me and calling my name, but before long I couldn't hear his voice. I stopped and wrenched myself around, but he was gone. I ran back, faster than I had ever run in my life, but he was nowhere to be found.

Every night I would wake up in a cold sweat, the room dark around me, and I'd force myself to stay awake until the warmth of dawn crept onto the horizon. My eyes bloodshot and my eyelids drooping, I watched old movies on mute in the living room to keep from falling asleep again. I put the coffee on to brew before Mom and Dad woke up.

The school counselors advised my parents to let me stay home for a while to get my bearings again. My parents left it to me to decide.

The morning of my first day back at school, I woke well ahead of sunrise, clutching my sheets with clammy hands. Instead of switching on the tv, I got coffee ready, poured a cup for myself, and took it to the office.

Monday, April 18, 2016

Mark is dead.

Mark. Little Marky Mark. I totally would have called him that, too, and he would have whined about it, and it would have been adorable.

Marky Mark, Big Sister misses you so much she can't stand it. I miss you so much, baby bro. I miss you so, so much. I want to hold your hands and kiss your toes and make you laugh and I'm dying inside thinking of how I'll never get to do any of it, how I never got to do any of it because you were stuck in a clear plastic coffin in a hospital before you even died.

I keep having the same nightmare about running from

him. I would never run from Mark. He looks so much like me in the dream. Mom has a picture of Mark on her phone, and he's as anglo as they come.

Was.

He was.

And now he's rotting into the ground, because whatever he needed to keep his precious little body alive wasn't there.

It could have been me. If I had died, there would have been no adoption, no questions for me to ask, no bio-mom wondering how I'm doing (or not), no adopted parents struggling to make their odd family work. Why wasn't it me, and not this little boy who had everything going for him—bio-parents who wanted him, and a whole happy life ahead of him?

If it had been me and not Mark, Mom and Dad wouldn't be going through all this pain, because they never would have come to know me in the first place. And it doesn't look like my bio-parents gave a crap about me anyway, did they? Or they wouldn't have given me up.

That story about Orphan Annie, where she imagines her

parents are just waiting for the tide to turn so they can come back for her? Bull.

You don't give up on your kids.

I'm furious. My parents were robbed of the baby they wanted so much, and my bio-mom just gave me up like I was nothing.

I've had all these questions up to this point, like if my bio-mom had kept me, would I have had brothers and sisters? Do I have bio-brothers and bio-sisters?

All my life, or at least ever since first grade when Cynthia pointed out how I was different from everyone else, I've wanted so much to find out who I really am. I love Mom and Dad, but for so long I've felt like there is more to me than them. But now I'm seeing the love of two parents for their dead child, and—all I can think of was that that part of me that was more, the family beyond my adoptive family, they just gave me up.

I want to know why. I need to know how I could have mattered so little to them that they could hand me off to people they didn't even know. I need to know the stories of where I came from, and I need to know what story made it okay for them to let me go.

I regret them ever creating me, just to leave me in this vacuum of unknowing and emptiness. I want them to see me and to see what they made my life into by turning their backs on me. It isn't right. IT ISN'T RIGHT.

I went and played ball yesterday. I took the bus. Didn't bother telling Mom or Dad. Just went. Coach couldn't believe what she was seeing when she saw me walk up, dressed and ready to go. I don't think anyone could believe it. And even Cynthia didn't say a word. Her eyes grew big, but she kept her mouth shut. Ariela came over and gave me a hug, but she didn't ask me anything or say anything. She knows. I warmed up with Tiffany who said a world of things without saying anything. Coach sat me for the first couple innings. She came up to me after that and said, "You sure you want to do this?" And I nodded, and my face grew hot and wet and horrible, but I went out there anyway, and to be honest, I sucked. Missed two outs at home when I was on defense and missed every at-bat, including the first two in the final inning. We were losing by one. One runner on first. I'd already gotten two strikes. And then I saw it--the pitcher saw she was about to win, and she laughed at me with her catcher, looking straight through me as if I were trash. In that moment, all of my fury crystalized into a single molten point. I wanted to hit her square in her pitcher's mask. She pitched, and I swung, adjusting at the last second to swing up. All the power of the last week and a half transferred from my bat to the ball, and with a solid POP that felt like nothing as I swung, the ball soared out of the park—for a walk-off win. I was in a haze as I rounded the diamond, my team screaming at me to touch 'em all. I did, and every last one of my teammates cheered and screamed for me as I crossed home. I fell to my knees after I crossed home. I couldn't see through my tears. I couldn't hear anything. I cried and cried. And then Ariela and Tiffany helped me up, and Tiffany's parents drove me home.

I'm claiming that hit for you, Marky Mark. And for every kid who was given up. Every kid like me.

I think I can hear Mom and Dad moving around. I guess it's time to go face the music.

"Medley, we got a call from your softball coach a few minutes ago."

I followed Mom's voice into the kitchen where she and Dad were sitting at the breakfast table, still in their bathrobes.

"I thought we agreed that you were going to take a break from all that for now," Mom continued. She sounded as tired as she looked. She had dark bags under her eyes and her eyes were red. I stopped a few feet from the breakfast table and folded my arms, leaning against the peach-colored wall.

"I wanted to play," I said.

"She asked why you were upset. How do you think it felt for me to have to tell someone we barely know about why you were upset?"

"I'm sorry. But you can't expect me to stay cooped up here forever being miserable. I needed to get all this—" I gestured around wildly. "—out of me. It's too much!"

Mom shook her head and put her face in her hands.

"People will have to learn sometime," I said.

Something on the floor caught my eye. It was a little dark

splotch near her heel where something sticky had caught the dust and never been washed away. Suddenly I wanted to grab a rag and scrub away every ugly thing that surrounded my family, but that small spot alone seemed insurmountable.

I heard Mom begin to cry softly. Dad reached over to rub her back, but she shrugged away. *All this pain at losing their flesh and blood,* I thought. *And my bio-mom just gave me away.*

I eyed the soft bread in its plastic sack on the counter next to the toaster, but my stomach felt queasy and my chest felt impossibly tight. I grabbed my water bottle instead, filled it with filtered water from the fridge, and called goodbye as I walked out the door.

Ariela stood at the corner at our first shared turn toward school. There was no Cynthia in sight, and Ariela had her gaze locked on me. The tightness in my chest increased. She held up a circlet of yellow oleander as I approached her, the same kind I'd made her when we were little and she was still Aaron and life wasn't a boulder of anger pinning me against a wall of grief.

Ariela looked as if she was going to hand the circlet to

me, but instead she set the circlet on my head and pressed her forehead against mine for a moment. My chest was a volcano, all molten pressure waiting to erupt. Time slowed as we stood there. She had no way of feeling the weight that threatened to crush me, but in that moment the pressure in my chest released slowly, steadily, in a trail of tears from my eyes. I didn't explain—I couldn't have if I had wanted to. It was too much to say.

I touched the soft blossoms on top of my head and brought my trembling fingers to my nose, taking a deep, shaky breath. I trembled, swallowing gulps of the scent.

We walked together step by step, side by side, without a word. Waterfalls continued to fall. The tightness in my chest eased as we moved. My mind was full, thinking of my little brother who would never grow up, thinking of my bio-parents who never parented me, and wondering how I was going to get through this endless day of stares and whispers.

Ariela squeezed me in a side-hug as we approached the school and then left me with a wave. I wiped my eyes. Just then, Tiffany appeared in the midst of the crowd and swooped through it to link arms with me. As she pulled me along, I felt the pressure in my chest building and squeezing the breath from me again, but she moved ahead with determination, weaving the two of us through swaths of students and teachers. She stopped at a locker three doors down from my own and spun the dial back and forth till the lock clicked open. I watched as she opened her locker door, carefully avoiding the curious looks of the seas of students walking by—and there, plastered along the back side of her locker, was an eight-by-ten glossy picture of me crossing home plate at our last game for the walk-off win. The picture was taken from the perspective of the team waiting behind homeplate. Long, out of focus ponytails and braids gained clarity, moving in the direction of my face, which was crisp, central to the photograph. I reached out for the photo and pulled it gently off her locker wall. In the photo I pointed my index finger toward the sky with my left hand and held my heart with my right. My hair cascaded behind me, shining in the bright stadium lights. My mouth was a wide "O," all teeth and roar. And there were my tears, betraying my secret.

Tiffany laid a hand on my left shoulder, pulling me gently

till I was fully facing her.

"We're with you, Medley," she said. Her eyes bore into mine with steady calm and fierce flame of energy that I couldn't name.

"Your team is here for you—you're one of us, and we're part of you, and there's nothing we won't do to help you. But the fact is, you've got everything you need right inside you. Just look at you. Look at yourself. We were just cheering you on. That?" She pointed at my face in the photo with a sports-length fingernail. "That is you tapping into all your love and anger and joy and sadness to launch your own unique power—the power to do whatever you choose. Whether it's winning a game for your team with a walk-off or dealing with unimaginable pain. You've got this, sister friend," she said in a hoarse whisper.

I held the photo against my chest and felt my heartbeat through it. Tiffany took it from my hands and peeled the tape off the back.

"You keep it," she said, handing it back. She pulled a pack of blue masking tape out of her backpack. "And this."

Her eyes were wells that reflected and held the shape of

my heart. I traced the face in the picture with my fingers, each line and curve as familiar as the seams of a ball. She hugged me, and monsoon rains fell between us in torrents.

Chapter 10

Mom and Dad spent the last Saturday of April packing up the baby's room. When I shuffled mid-yawn from my room to the kitchen that morning, I caught sight of Dad carrying parts of the dissembled crib to the garage. I peeked in and saw Mom peeling decals of teddy bears, balloons, and ABCs off the walls. They didn't invite me in or ask for my help. They worked steadily in silence.

The tension grew thick. I took a novel from the office and went out back to read. By noon the gentle morning breeze had become an uncomfortable heat. I went inside. Mom and Dad were finishing up. I paused at the edge of the doorway to look inside. The evidence of what it had been prepared for was gone. Four barren walls, a laminate wood floor, and handprints in the dust remained. Mom and Dad emerged. They shut the door behind them. Mom went to her room to shower; Dad went to the kitchen. I followed him. He wiped his face with a dish towel and poured himself a glass of water. He opened the morning edition of the *Arizona Republic*, but his gaze crossed over the paper and out the window. I made myself a sandwich for lunch. I took it to the office and closed the door, completing my family's triune isolation.

I considered switching on the computer to journal. Instead I sat in the desk chair and allowed my eyes to wander the walls and their floor to ceiling bookshelves. The small section that had been set aside for pregnancy and child-rearing books had been cleared, I noticed. My eyes wandered the desk's contents. Folders and papers were stacked high on one corner of the desk, and one folder caught my eye because it had my name on it in the tight, familiar writing of my mother. I picked up the folder. There were numerous papers pertaining to me— my vaccination record, old report cards, newspaper clippings of my state wins with my Little League team. My birth certificate was there, but then I realized it wasn't mine—it had someone else's name on it. I looked for mine in the rest of the folder, but it wasn't there.

The hair prickled on the back of my neck. I looked at the date of birth. It was my birthday. I eyed the name on the birth certificate more closely: Wipismal Zepeda.

I caught sight of the names of the mother and father. Not Melissa and Brian Blunt. The line for the father's name was blank. The name in the mother's blank was blacked out.

I stared, absorbing the details of the certificate.

Wipismal Zepeda?

I traced the strange name with trembling fingers. My heart thumped, and I stole glances at the door, expecting one of my parents to burst in and discover me discovering this pounding drum of a secret. I allowed the shape of each letter of each name to burn itself into my memory.

I closed the folder and set it back with the stack of papers I'd found it on. I opened the office door as quietly as I could, stepped out of the office, and hurried down to my room, closing the door behind me. Wide-eyed, heart racing, I turned toward my mirror.

There stood the fatherless girl whose mother had no name. But the girl had a name.

"Wipismal," I whispered.

The girl with the shining black hair, not-pale skin, and fiery demeanor, the girl who had worked her way to the Little League state tournament win with her best friend and was fighting her way pitch by pitch to glory as a softball player, the girl who wove words and defied convention, the girl who had never looked like her parents, the girl whose baby brother was dead, the girl who might have blood siblings and a blood mother as near as a city away—that girl staring back in the mirror was named Wipismal.

I turned from the mirror, wiping and then fanning my face. Sucking in a long breath, I opened my door and walked down the hall, through the dining room and living room, out onto the now sweltering hot deck, and lifted myself over the wall. I didn't bother knocking as I slipped inside Ariela's house. Her mother looked up in surprise from her couch, and I stopped, remembering my manners, and also remembering a beat late that this was their sabbath day.

"*Shabbat Shalom*, Mrs. Spieler," I said.

"*Shabbat Shalom*, Medley. Are you looking for Aaron?"

"Yeah. Is that okay? It's kind of important."

Ariela's mom nodded. "Sure. Is everything okay?"

I nodded as I walked to Ariela's room. "Everything's fine," I said over my shoulder.

Ariela looked up in surprise when I burst into her room and closed the door behind me. She was wearing a thin white tank and soccer shorts. She also had a long, white, blue-striped cloth with long tassels wrapped around her and a *yarmulke* on her head. She had a book propped up against her knees. When she set the book down, I saw it was a copy of *Torah*. I had interrupted her *Shabbat* reading.

"Aw, crap. This is not a good time," I muttered, shaking my head.

I turned and reached for the door handle, but Ariela said "Wait!" in a loud whisper.

She jumped up and came over, placing her hand lightly on the door to keep me from leaving. She motioned for me to stay quiet, listened at the door for a moment, and then pulled me toward her desk and gestured for me to sit down.

"What's going on?" she asked, her eyes fixed on me.

I blinked back another wave of tears.

"I can't talk about it here," I said in a hoarse voice. "Can you come with me?"

Ariela glanced at the door and then at her Torah. "We have dinner at sundown, right around seven. I need to be back for that. Where are we going?"

"Can you pull something up on your phone?" I said in a low voice.

Ariela handed me her smartphone and I began typing in the maps app.

"Here," I said.

Ariela looked at her phone and then at me, a question mark etched on her face.

"You coming?" I asked.

She went to her chest of drawers and pulled out long pants and a t-shirt. "I'll have to borrow a bike from your house—I'm not supposed to ride on *Shabbat*, and I'm assuming you don't intend to walk."

She turned to get dressed, and I turned my face to the wall. My excitement and fear grew as I waited, thinking about what I was about to do. In the space of a minute Ariela had clothes and sneakers pulled on.

"Leave the talking to me," Ariela whispered before opening the door.

"Mom, Medley and I are going to go for a walk. I'll be back before dinner. Is that okay?" Ariela said.

"Bring some water with you, okay? It's warmed up out there," Mrs. Spieler said.

Ariela gave her mom a kiss. We grabbed water bottles from their fridge and then scooted out their front door. A few minutes later, we were in my garage, grabbing bicycles. I rolled the bikes out quickly, wondering if one of my parents was going to open the door from the kitchen to garage and ask what we were doing, but they didn't. With helmets retrieved for each of us, I punched the button to close the garage door and we rode off. I leaned hard left to go north up Price, the frontage road next to the 101 highway. I could hear Ariela breathing hard as she pedaled behind me.

When we reached the intersection of Price and Broadway, the first major intersection on our route, we slowed to a stop for the red light. Westward I saw tall trees, leafy green with the end of spring and oranges littered along the sidewalks.

Ariela swigged some water and looked my way. "What is this about, Medley?"

I shook my head and pointed a single finger north. The light turned green, and I began to pedal straight ahead. A couple of minutes later, we rolled through a green light at Price and Apache. The light rail train beeped two quick high-pitched beeps to the east of us, warning of its approach. A couple of minutes after that, we caught another green light at Price and University. During our ride the residential neighborhoods turned to generic shopping centers full of specialty shops. We continued on, and at Price and Rio Salado, the only option was to turn east or west. Turning west would take us toward Tempe Marketplace, an upscale outdoor mall, Arizona State University, home to tens of thousands of college students, and Mill Avenue, one of the oldest streets in Tempe.

Instead, we turned east, riding past the Cubs spring training stadium, Sloan Park, and then past Riverview Park, which was currently packed with kids and parents playing at the water and on the playgrounds. We rode past several shopping plazas where car dealerships, restaurants, and stores sprawled, a map of wealth acquired and spent. We could have turned north on Dobson into the labyrinth of Riverview Mall, but instead kept going toward Alma School Road where the traffic was lighter. We turned north, crossing under the 202 and over the Salt River to McKellips and on toward McDowell. The landscape here was less developed and gave a glimpse of what the desert was like before carefully planned housing associations became the Valley of the Sun's main cash crop. This was the Salt River reservation, an expanse thick with stillness and whispers of memory next to all the hurry and modern glitz of Phoenix and its carefully gridded suburbs.

One more mile, and we were at Thomas Road. We turned west toward Scottsdale, home of the much-much-richer-than-everyone-else. Professional athletes and their front-row fans lived there, along with winter and spring-time migrants from wealthy quarters all over the country. We turned north on Longmore less than a mile from Alma School Road before getting too deep into Scottsdale, and before long we were pulling up next to our destination.

Ariela squeaked to a stop next to me as I looked at an enclosed dome structure before us. It looked as if it had been crafted by hand. Beyond it was the Huhugam Ki Museum.

Ariela drank some of her water, and I realized I was parched and very warm. I opened my water bottle and began to drink.

"Save some for the ride home, girlfriend. You're not going to last," Ariela said. Her eyes betrayed her concern, but her voice remained calm.

I took off my helmet and fished in my pockets for a hair tie. I found one and then pulled my hair up into a ponytail. The breeze cooled my neck, tickling it softly. I dismounted from my bike and rolled it into the shade. Ariela followed.

"So are you planning to tell me why I'm rolling through Scottsdale on *Shabbat*?" Ariela said.

I held a finger up to my mouth and approached the entrance to the museum. I paused.

I touched the wrought iron door handle, but quickly withdrew my hand. The handle was hot. Ariela looked quizzically at me. I took a breath and flung open the door.

The scent of an earthy, unfamiliar incense greeted me from the cool interior. I walked inside, greeted by images of people who looked like me. I hesitated a moment at the door. A docent with straight, silver-threaded hair and kind eyes greeted me.

"Welcome. What brings you here, young lady?"

I opened my mouth. Then I closed it. Ariela put a hand on my shoulder.

"I came here without my parent's permission, and I'm sure they wouldn't want me to be here," I said, weighing my words.

"Why would they not want you to be here?" she queried.

"Because... because...."

I swallowed. Fear of the consequences of telling the truth gripped me.

I took a deep breath, and answered in a low voice, "Because I think I was born on this reservation, and my parents don't know that." Ariela inhaled sharply. The docent's eyes remained fixed on mine.

"What is your name?" she asked quietly.

"Med-" I began, but I stopped.

"My name is...."

I stopped again, my heart pounding like a drum.

"My name..." I began again, "...is Wipismal. Wipismal Zepeda."

Chapter 11

Wipismal," she breathed. Her eyes looked as if they might hold the knowledge of the entire reservation. There was more than knowledge in her eyes. I perceived recognition. I stared at her with a thousand questions, but I couldn't think of a single word to say.

All my secrets were revealed in her glance.

"Come," the woman said, "let us sit together. You look tired and thirsty."

I gathered that she knew more about the nature of my thirst than Ariela could imagine. I linked fingers with Ariela and pulled her along.

The woman led us through a curtained doorway and gestured for us to have a seat at a half-moon wooden table with three chairs set against a pale, cream-colored wall. A large labyrinth with a figure approaching its entrance hung from the wall. I took the far chair and Ariela took the one closest to the threshold. The woman busied herself with pouring two glasses of water from a water cooler. She set them before us and we thanked her before gulping them down. Meanwhile, she ascended a small footstool to reach a tin at the top of a tall bookshelf. Back at the table, she opened the tin and the smell of gingersnaps filled the room.

"I just made these," she said.

Ariela declined, but I took one. It was soft, slightly warm, and melted in my mouth. Ariela raised her eyebrows at me. I shrugged.

"Do you know one other?" Ariela asked us.

"We just met," I said through a mouthful of cookie.

"Actually, that's not quite true," the woman said.

I began to cough. Ariela jumped up and pounded me on the back. I held up my empty water glass. The woman hurried to refill it. After a sip, I took a ragged breath and coughed some more.

"What do you mean, that's not quite true?" I asked.

"Hang on a moment," she said. She stood and exited the

curtained room, leaving us alone.

While she was gone, Ariela whispered, "What are we *doing* here? Who is this lady?"

"I found something this morning," I whispered back.

The woman passed the threshold with what looked like an old-fashioned photo album, the kind with firm pages covered in thin lines of adhesive and protected by sheets of cellophane. She set it in front of me and opened it, flipping through the pages until she found the one she was looking for. Ariela leaned in to get a look. It was a picture of a baby, tiny as a baby doll, being held in its mother's arms.

I stared at the picture of the mother. She was a little older than me. Her dark hair went past her hips. She wore a white dress with no sleeves, and there was some kind of symmetrical pattern on it—the center of it had a vertical diamond. She wore a necklace of silver and gemstones. The stones looked like they could have been turquoise, but the picture was black and white. Her face was solemn as she stared into the camera.

Ariela turned the book so she could see it, and her eyes grew wide. "That woman looks just like you, Medley."

I looked back at Ariela. My heart raced.

"That woman is the one who gave you birth," she said. "And I was her midwife."

She laid a weathered hand on my forehead and began to speak quietly in a lilting language I did not know. Shocked, I sat still, drinking in the words of this woman's people—of my mother's people. I closed my eyes, and wisps of forgotten memory swirled in my mind's eye. Soon the woman fell quiet again, and I opened my eyes. Ariela stared, her eyes shifting from me to the woman and back again.

"Would you like to meet your family?" she asked me.

The wish of a thousand dreams crashed onto the shore of the here and now.

But then anger rose from the waves like a hurricane. If they were this close to me all this time, why hadn't they come to find me? Why had they waited for me to make the first move?

"Why did my mother give me up?" I demanded.

She looked at me with what looked like sympathy. My anger swelled, threatening to burst like horses into a stampede, leveling the room and everyone in it. Before she could answer, her gaze turned at the sound of the front door swinging open and shut, and footsteps clicking down the hallway.

"Good morning," a female voice called. Ariela and I turned. A tall woman with sleek black and silver hair, brown skin, and smile lines glanced at us briefly before settling on the priest.

"I'm sorry, I didn't realize you were seeing visitors. I just came by...." Her voice trailed off as her eyes met mine again. She searched my face, and her own eyes grew wide. The world magnified and closed in on us as we beheld one another, mirrors of one another.

I jumped from my chair and ran past the woman and out the door, down the steps, and onto my bike.

"Medley, wait!" Ariela called, but I did not wait.

I pedaled away as hard and fast as I could, ignoring everything but the wind whipping my ponytail against my body and the pain that seared my calves as I tore down the road from which I had come.

Neither woman attempted to follow us, and I eased my pace once I crossed over the Salt River. Ariela caught up to me at an intersection in Mesa, but I did not look at her. I could feel her questions hanging in the air, but she did not ask them, and I did not offer an answer. What was there to say?

It wasn't yet noon when we rode past the sign for the Villas at Shandalay. She rode up with me to my garage door, and I pressed the code to open it. She rolled the bike in and pushed down the kickstand. I followed. Before she left, she hugged me tight, letting her questions go unanswered.

I poured a glass of cold water in the kitchen, swallowing it down without taking a breath. I set the glass in the sink, then headed for my room to get out of my clothes. Several minutes later, I stepped into the shower and let the warm water wash away the dust, sweat, and tears that had gathered all over me. The aches in my legs eased, but the pain in my chest pulsed. I turned the shower off when my tears ran out.

In my room, I dressed in soft leggings and a t-shirt. I combed my dripping hair with my fingers, wondering if the woman with the smile lines did the same after washing her hair.

I didn't know what to do, so I sat on the edge of my bed and looked in my bedroom mirror. I was a reflection of the woman from the newspaper clipping, the woman who had also walked in to the backroom of the museum without announcing herself. My blood mother was alive and well, a bike-ride from where I had lived my whole life. I sought comfort in today's answers to my old questions, but new questions surrounded me like an itchy blanket.

She didn't even come after me. She recognized me, and she didn't try to keep me there.

A knock at my bedroom door made me jump.

"Come in," I said.

My dad opened the door a crack. "Medley, it's dinnertime. Would you please set the table?"

"Sure, Dad."

He left the door open for me. I slid off the bed and headed into the kitchen. Mom was there, slicing carrots, a frown on her face. I touched her arm. She paused. I wrapped my arms around her, burying my nose in her neck, hugging her from behind. She set the knife down and lifted her hands to hold mine. I took a deep breath, breathing in the soft scent of her perfume, Wings, which she'd worn since I was a small girl. *This is my mother.*

"What is this for?" she said, pulling away to turn and look at me. Her eyes revealed sadness lined with curiosity.

"I love you, Mama," I whispered. "I'm sorry you lost Mark. I know you wanted him so much."

"More than you can possibly imagine, my sweet. We wanted him as much as we wanted you."

Mom's eyes were wet. I stared into the eyes of a woman who had always wanted me, had always loved me, and had never given up on me. Yet this woman did not share my blood and had never told me who or where I had come from. This woman had done the best she could. She had withheld who I was, perhaps thinking she was protecting me, and then made a new story to go in my story's place. Her love had always longed to protect me, but she could not protect me from my desire to know myself.

I rested my head on her shoulder and hugged her again, wishing I'd never seen what rested on my parents' desk this morning. But now I knew, and my choice was made. I had to return and find out who I was—my curiosity was too great to do otherwise. And I couldn't breathe a word of it to the family who had made a life for me.

Dad came over and tousled my hair. Mom smoothed it with a chuckle and then wiped my cheeks dry with the back of her hand.

"Why don't you set the table," she said.

I pressed my forehead to hers before I turned to the cupboard to pull out plates for our meal. As I passed by, Mom cupped the carrot slices and sprinkled them over the salad of romaine and red leaf lettuce she had prepared. I set three places at our dining room table, walking past the still-fresh memory of my mom lying on the floor in a pool of her own blood. Dad came in with a bowl of steaming wheat linguine and heaped some onto each plate. Mom set the salad bowl and dressing on the table as Dad went to the kitchen, and as she turned, he returned to the table to ladle my favorite spaghetti sauce, tuna with lemon zest and capers, onto each pile of pasta. My mouth watered, and a pang of gratitude overshadowed by guilt flooded me. I couldn't reveal to them where I'd been or why I'd gone. Telling them the truth, that I wanted to know my biological family, would be too much for them.

After dinner, Mom headed to her bathroom for an early bath, and Dad settled on the couch to read the newspaper. With an hour or so left of the day, the golden hour was upon us. I slipped onto the deck with my walkie talkie and hit the send button. "Wanna throw the ball?"

A staticky reply came through. "Sure."

I told Dad where I was going, put on my sneakers, grabbed my ball and glove, and walked down the street to where Ariela was waiting for me, glove tucked in her armpit, arms crossed.

"You going to tell me?" Ariela said

I threw the ball hard with my left hand. Ariela's arms uncrossed like lightning. She caught the ball.

"You're the only person I can tell. And I need your help."

Ariela returned the ball, aiming straight at my chest. I caught the ball with the web of my glove, narrowly avoiding a vicious sting to my palm.

"I miss playing ball with you," I said, returning the ball, underhanded this time.

"What kind of help are you looking for?" she said,

returning the ball with a side-arm throw.

I took a few steps back so I could put more power behind the next one. I heaved it at Ariela. She caught it.

"I need to know who my family is. My biological family. I need to know who I am."

Ariela underhanded the ball back to me. I nearly lost it in the sun, but swiped it a few inches above the pavement.

"I have no idea where I came from, apart from what little I found out today. I need to know who I was born to be."

I threw a lightning bolt. Ariela caught it and held it. I waited, ready.

"I think I know what you mean," Ariela said.

She threw the ball back. I caught it with a leap. Ariela approached me slowly, taking her glove off as she walked.

"Look, Medley. I don't understand what today was all about. But I will help you, because you're my friend. I just need you to trust me enough to tell me what's going on. Don't just ride off into the morning without breathing a word of it to me, okay? I'm here for you, and I need you to help me help you."

I nodded. The dam of tears threatened to burst again.

Ariela turned her head back, gesturing for us to walk toward her house.

"So let me make sure I've got everything straight so far," she said. "That woman was the midwife at your birth. Yes?"

"Apparently."

"And that woman who came in was the same woman in the picture, yes?"

"So it seems."

"So that makes that woman your mother, and the older woman helped bring you into the world, and your real name is...."

"Wipismal," I said.

Ariela stopped, pulling on my hand to stop me. I turned to face her.

"That's a lot to learn in one day," she said softly.

I lifted my chin and gave a firm nod.

"Hey, you listened to me tell you that I wasn't actually a boy. You could try to out-shock me, but you'd probably fail, so."

I snorted, my steely face melting into a grin.

I tossed the ball straight up with my left hand. Ariela

clasped my right hand in her left as we continued walking down the street. I gripped the ball and glanced down.

"Dude, what if someone sees us?" I asked.

"Sees what?" Ariela turned to me.

"You know what we look like right now."

"Since when do you care what you look like?"

I let go of her hand, the events of the morning pounding in my head. I thought of my bio-mother. "Since today."

Ariela turned to me. "So it's okay for you to be girly, just not with me?"

I paused, taken aback. "Since when do I hold hands with any of my friends?"

We looked at each other for a long moment.

"It's a pretty girly thing to do, walking hand in hand," she said, turning her gaze to the ground.

"Public service announcement: I'm not very girly," I said.

Ariela paused, looking at the ground, and then started walking again. I looked after her and then hurried to catch up.

"Hey, there are lots of ways to be a girl. If you wanna be girly with a friend, you just need to find a girly friend to be girly with."

"I only have you, Medley."

"But I'm not girly, Ariela."

"Holding hands isn't a huge deal for girls. What difference does it make?" Ariela asked, her tone laced with emotion I couldn't identify.

"Because the only reason I'd hold the hand of someone our age is if I want to go out with them. Besides, what would Cynthia think? Also, I thought you were supposed to be the one who's preoccupied with what image you project to the world? As far as the rest of the world knows, you're still a boy."

Ariela shook her head.

"Hey," I said, quietly this time. "I'm going to tell you something I heard from a wise person: you're still my best friend. That's not going to change, no matter what else may happen. I just... maybe I can't be everything you need. And maybe you can't be everything I need. And maybe you'll— maybe we'll both—find what we need if we keep looking."

Ariela looked at my hands. "Sorry. That was weird. I shouldn't have taken your hand like that, not without asking you first. Especially when today's already been one of the weirdest days of your life."

I let out a long breath. "It's okay. And hey, a whole lot of boys would never have said sorry. Seems like your transition into girldom is going just fine."

"We're both going to get where we're going." She'd said the same thing right before we won the Little League state tournament.

"Right now I'd say you're headed...." I looked down the street and flung the ball ahead of us as hard as I could. "...that way."

We looked at each other for a moment before breaking into a run toward my flyaway ball.

That night, when I switched off my bedside lamp, the conversation between Ariela and me unfolded in my memory's eye.

It felt strange to say no to my best friend. She was exploring who she was as a girl, and I'd said no to her when she tried something new.

But she still has to ask if it's okay with me. Especially since her current romantic interest is a girl, and she's still choosing to present herself in public as a boy.

I thought of how I'd dragged her out of the house without telling her where we were going or why.

But she agreed to go.

Also, I don't need to own her journey. She does.

But how can someone go on a journey like that without tremendous support from her friends? I don't know if I'd have been able to make my journey up north without her support.

Nana's voice sounded in my mind, velvety and soft. *You would have if you'd had to. She's consented every step along the way, even when she hasn't known what's going on. And her consent is the difference. Both of you need to be more mindful of whether you've asked if something is okay, and you both ought to be mindful of whether or not you're okay with what's happening. There's nothing wrong with saying no.*

My birth mother's face came to mind—her startled look, the recognition that flashed in her eyes, the way her body seemed to make way as I ran past within inches of her.

And what if my bio-mom says she can't be what I need her to be, Nana?

Hot tears stung my eyes. I buried my face in my pillow and wept until darkness covered me.

Chapter 12

I speared the ball to Tiffany in warm-ups the next day, my ponytail whipping through the air. Tiffany's hair was arranged in two tight French braids that joined as a single braid over her left shoulder. The smell of clay, leather, and sweat curled around us. We would play against the Eagles today. Their record this season had so far proven them to be one of the best teams in the league. The sun blazed down on us as we whipped the ball back and forth.

Tiffany threw the ball near the dirt, and I crouched to catch it. It landed in the webbing of my glove, and my feet turned as I swept my glove around and behind me, tagging the imaginary homeplate at my heel.

Tiffany let out a low whistle. "They'll have a surprise waiting for them if they try to run on you," she said.

A couple of minutes before the game, Coach called us all

into a huddle. Cynthia wiggled her fingers, her nails bright red but trimmed short, in the direction of the stands. I looked over and saw Ariela sitting in the shade behind our dugout. She wore sunglasses and sat motionless, elbows back on the bench behind her. She smiled as I looked in her direction. I waved before turning back.

"Ladies, lean in. This is going to be our toughest game yet," Coach said. "The Eagles are an outstanding team. Their weakness is their batting, but what they lack in hitting they make up for on the base path. Also, their defense is top-notch: their pitchers don't give up many runs, and their outfield rarely gives a free bag, so we need to play just as smart. No freebies, wait for a good pitch, and watch your base coaches. Are you ready to fly?"

We crossed our arms right over left and linked hands. On the count of three, we lifted our arms over our heads, turned in place with hands still linked, and shouted, "Hummingbirds!"

We were the home team, so we scattered to our defensive positions. As I put on my pads and looked around, I caught sight of Ariela again. This time she was shuffling through the bleachers to sit down next to my parents. I couldn't remember if they had been to one of my games yet this season. My mom gave Ariela a hug and gestured for her to sit down next to her. Dad shook her hand. Mom saw me and waved, her lips moving with a smile as she pointed me out to Dad. He gave me a thumbs-up. The first batter approached, so I pulled on my face-mask and crouched into position. My family's world had come undone in the midst of this softball season, but here I was, still working through the transition from baseball star to softball player. The first batter took some warm-up swings as I signaled to Cynthia to pitch low and inside. *I wonder if anyone else's life has changed like mine has in the last two months.*

The first couple of innings we held them to a single run. Cynthia's pitching was on-point. Only one runner from the Eagles made it to first base, and she attempted to steal second when the batter behind her hit a can of corn in the air. She would have been safe if she had stayed at second, but she rounded to third. I caught the ball and hurled it to Tiffany at third, who caught it and tagged out the runner for the third out of the inning. Our fans let out whoops from the bleachers; I screamed and ran to Tiffany to high-five her. The rest of the team swatted both of us with their gloves as we congregated in the dugout.

"Medley, you're up!" Coach called, and I hurried to switch out my catcher's gear for my batting gloves and bat.

The Eagles pitcher, a tall girl with sand-colored skin and a steely jaw, stared in my direction, unblinking as the catcher behind me motioned for a pitch. The pitcher turned and set before winding her arm in a lighting fast pitch. My swing was in the right place, but it was a full second behind the ball. This girl could *throw*.

The catcher threw the ball back. I shrugged my shoulders back and took a couple of easy swings before setting up again. This time I swung early, but the pitcher anticipated me, throwing a full ten miles an hour slower, and I was ahead of the ball by half a second. I swore under my breath. My team called out encouragement. My parents called my name as they clapped, and I turned to look at them before setting up for my next swing. I thought I saw someone familiar.

Is that...?

My hands felt clammy. I gulped back my nerves and took a deep breath before turning back to the pitcher. She didn't wait; she pitched the ball and I swung hard.

"Out!" cried the umpire.

I turned back as Hummingbird fans cried "Ohh" in disappointment. My biological mother, who had appeared just a moment ago, was nowhere to be seen.

"We'll get them on the next one. No worries," Cynthia said as we passed each other.

I looked at her in surprise. Ariela met me at the outer entrance to the dugout.

"What?" Ariela said, following my gaze to where mine rested on Cynthia, who was approaching the plate.

"Your girlfriend was nice to me," I said.

"No—before you batted. You looked like you'd seen a ghost."

"I thought I saw someone—" My voice trailed off as I looked around the bleachers again.

"Thought you saw who?" Mom asked, catching me off-guard. I blinked and saw my mom and dad standing to my left.

They looked concerned.

"Nobody. Just someone I thought I met recently. Probably a trick of the sun."

Ariela raised an eyebrow but said nothing else.

"Don't let that last at-bat get to you, slugger," Dad said.

"Yep—remember what we've taught you. Just breathe through it. There's a lot more game left to be played," Mom said.

I had already taken off my batting gloves and was ready to put on my catcher's gear, but instead I entered the dugout and leaned against the fence to watch the remainder of the inning play out.

Sunday, May 1, 2016

I stood face-to-face with my birth mother yesterday.

I was sitting in here in the office when I found a folder with my birth certificate. The line for the mother's name was blacked out, and there was no name at all in the space given for the father. The line for my name said "Wipismal Zepeda." The date of birth was mine.

I dragged Ariela out with me to the Salt River

reservation. We rode our bikes there. We went to the Huhugam Ki Museum. The woman we met behind the desk knew me by my birthname. She told me she was the midwife at my birth. Then a woman walked in. She recognized me the moment I recognized her. I ran out. I couldn't face my bio-mom. Not like that.

Then today my softball team played against the Eagles, the best team in our league, and at the start of the third inning I turned and thought I saw her for a moment, but after I struck out, she was gone.

I want to go back, maybe next Saturday. I can tell Mom and Dad I want to go to Shabbat with Ariela. They won't hassle me. And Ariela won't tell.

In other news, there are a couple weeks of games left in the softball season. We lost against the Eagles today, but as Coach told us after our shuttle runs, we have a shot to go to the playoffs. So there's that. I had a pretty awesome shot to Tiffany at third to end the second inning. We're still in this.

Things with Ariela got weird yesterday. After we got back from Scottsdale, she called me on the walkie talkie to see if I wanted to play catch. So I went out there, and we're throwing the ball, and I talked a bit with her about what happened up north, and then she grabbed my hand as we were walking down the street. It caught me off guard, and I became self-conscious. Her holding my hand felt completely off.

The great thing, though? I told her I wasn't comfortable, and she apologized. She didn't belittle me, she didn't harass me. She said she was sorry for crossing the boundary I was setting. In a world full of dudes who feel completely at liberty to treat females however they wish, Ariela knows how to treat females, and how to step back when she's wrong. She's doing just fine as a girl. Not that my opinion about her success as a girl really holds any weight whatsoever. There are lots of ways to be a girl, including being a jerk (hello, Cynthia). So I guess I should say as her friend, and as a fellow human being, I think Ariela's doing just fine.

I'm grateful for Ariela. She rode up to Scottsdale with me even though I didn't tell her what was going on. She didn't go off on me when I left her pretty much in the dust up there when I saw my bio-mom and bolted. I need to find some way to thank her.

Maybe I can start trying to be nicer to Cynthia. I'd rather have as little to do with her as possible, but Ariela likes her. She likes her a lot. And I'm sure Ariela would appreciate knowing that I wasn't deliberately giving Cynthia the cold shoulder.

Man, the things we do for our friends.

I dunno if Cynthia is worth anything, but Ariela absolutely is worth it. She's the best friend a girl could want.

Let's do this.

Chapter 13

Have you given thought to what you want to write for your piece for the last issue of the year, Medley?"

I looked up from my blank computer screen. It was the first Tuesday of the month in the final month of the school year, which meant I had about a week to figure out what to write. Next year we'd be starting again—I might do this column again, or I might do something else. One way or the other, I was planning to return, and I was hoping I'd end up with Ms. Feliz as my English teacher.

"I'm not sure," I said to Ms. Feliz. "I'm not sure what religious holidays come up in May, to be honest. Since it's the end of the year, it would be nice to find a holiday that honors coming full circle...." I tapped the keyboard lightly, willing a sentence to materialize on the screen before me.

"You've looked at Christian and Jewish holidays so far.

What are some other faiths you can think of that are represented here in Arizona?"

I shrugged. "I mean... there are the native peoples of Arizona. They honor each full moon, don't they?" I thought of my bio-mother, and of my name. I realized I had no idea what holy days the people of my birth might celebrate.

"I think you're onto something," Ms. Feliz said. "Why don't you dig around and see what you can find on the internet and go from there."

I can do more than that, I thought.

That Saturday, after a Thursday win against the Slugs that squeaked us into the playoffs as the number four seed, I told my parents I was going to the Shabbat evening service with Ariela followed by dinner. I rode my bike out of the open garage and pedaled hard northward toward Scottsdale, my heart racing as I rode ahead. *Will I see her again?*

When I arrived about an hour later, there were half a dozen people milling around the museum talking. With a couple of exceptions, everyone I saw looked like me—long, straight, glossy black hair, not-cream-colored skin. A couple of them did a double-take as I walked by. I kept moving. I detected the scent of a spice burning from inside the museum as I approached the door. It had a savory, weighty scent. Inside, I saw a couple of kids my age or a little younger tapping on hand drums. They had matching plaits running down their backs. They were talking and laughing in a language I didn't understand. I wondered if they were twins.

Then I saw her—my mother emerged from a back room. She wore a sleeveless white V-neck cotton blouse and a full turquoise, red, white, and black printed skirt that accentuated her graceful steps as she walked. I stood motionless, mesmerized by her.

Laughter and conversation swelled in the space. A drum sounded from another doorway. The drummer, a young woman, set a rhythmic pace, turning her body this way and that. The woman who had been midwife to my mother entered bearing a shallow, wide shell with a burning, pale green bundle of leaves in one hand and a large brown feather with a pale tip in the other. She flicked the feather in a circular motion and those she passed beckoned the smokey blessing with their hands. The midwife chanted in a language I did not recognize. I hesitated, feeling like an intruder, a violator of sacred space. The ceremony went on despite me. I closed my eyes, willing myself to remember the smells, sounds, and pulse of this place.

The unfamiliar words of my mother's native language washed over me, bidding me to remember an identity I had never known. The ritual actions grounded me, binding me to the identity of the community in a way that did not require words, despite the plethora of them.

All of it was familiar and strange at once. This was not my home, but I was at home. Chills fell and rose on my spine and cascaded across my arms. Every sensation was heightened in this place, by these people. The effect was dizzying.

At the ceremony's end, my mother stood again.

"On Saturday, June 4, we will have our annual summer full moon sweat lodge ceremony to welcome the fullness of what is, invite what is to come, and release what no longer gives life. All are invited. See me for details."

I blinked. *This is my chance.*

I didn't stay to talk to my bio-mother, and I didn't wait

to speak again with the midwife. Instead I slipped out the door, hopped on my bike, and raced home as the golden hour sent vibrant hues of light across the Valley of the Sun. I caught sight of Ariela and her parents walking back from *shul* as I neared my house, and I waved. They waved back. I rolled my bike back in the garage and entered the house through the kitchen. Dad remarked on how sweaty I was.

"It's hot out. Can you believe they walk to their synagogue every Sabbath, even in summer?"

Dad shook his head, and I withdrew to the office.

Saturday, May 7, 2016

I went back to the museum today and I found out my bio-mom is leading a sweat lodge ceremony at the next full moon, which is in a month. All are invited, she said.

I'm going to do it. I'm going to meet her, face to face.

I'm terrified.

But I'm going to do it.

And I need to figure out everything I can about sweat lodges before then. Apparently they're used for full moon ceremonies (or at least this full moon ceremony), so I have the perfect excuse to do some research.

The Hummingbirds beat the Slugs on Thursday which gives us the number four-spot in the playoffs. If we win tomorrow against the Eagles, we go to the championship game the following week.

If we don't win, we'll probably go out for an end of season farewell ice cream social. I don't have time for that if I'm going to make it to the library before it closes at 5:00pm.

So I guess I have one more reason to win.

I'm pretty sure if I can knock the socks off Coach Marge in general, I've got a solid future in softball ahead of me. And they need someone playing gauche to throw the other teams off their game.

Gauche was one of the words on my vocab list in English this week. It means awkward, inelegant, or socially unsophisticated. But the root comes from the French for "left," as in left-handed, which I am.

Might as well play to my strengths.

It was already uncomfortably warm as we threw pitches to one another on the softball field the next week. Out-of-staters would hardly last a minute in the stands; as it was, it was a clear, bright day, with almost no breeze to cut the heat. What breeze we did get felt like a blow dryer rather than a fan. This could be a long game.

We were up against the Eagles for Week 1 of the playoffs. Unsurprisingly, they secured the number one seed. The winner of this game would go on to play the winner of the Ladybugs v. Slugs game, who were the number two and three seeds, respectively. They would be playing immediately after this game. Part of me wanted to stay to watch the second game just in case the Ladybugs won, since they were the only team we hadn't played this season.

As if reading my mind, Coach Marge called us into a huddle just before gametime and said, "Listen, ladies, I know you might be thinking about next week already. Don't. Focus on the here and now, and give it your all. As we know, the Eagles are a great team, and we're not going to beat them without giving them every bit of focus we've got. Stay sharp, guard your territory, edge out theirs, and play to win. One, two, three."

"HUMMINGBIRDS!" we shouted together.

The Eagles were hosting us, so we returned to the dugout. Cynthia discarded her mitt for her batting gloves and bat and headed out to the batter's box. While Coach called out the lineup, we settled in against the chain link fence.

Cynthia started strong with a soaring ball to the fence on her first pitch that got her a stand-up double. The Hummingbirds let out large whoops—even I jumped and pumped my fist—as the catcher of the Eagles stood to talk to the pitcher. *It's always a good sign when the other team's pitcher is rattled—at first pitch, no less.*

We went through the entire lineup that first inning, racking up five runs along with a couple of outs. When I got up to the plate, Gwennie Lightfoot was on third. All I needed was a base hit and it would be a run batted in, and we could continue the inning from the top of our lineup. I heard a chorus of voices, including Ariela's and my parents', cheering my name. I got up to bat and tried to focus on the moment, like Coach had said. I heard people cheering for Gwennie behind me and glanced back. Was that my mother there? My eyes bulged and I turned back quickly. I took a breath and looked at the pitcher. She swung her arm and the ball flew at me. I swung belt-high, but the ball sank below my swing. Strike one.

I took a breath and centered myself, thinking of Little League and the state tournament last year. *Why didn't I stay in baseball?* I asked myself, not for the first time. The second pitch soared at me. I held my bat. Ball one. *That's more like it*, I thought, as I heard calls of "Good eye!" from the stands.

This time I didn't take my eyes or focus off the pitcher. I was a hummingbird guarding her territory. The pitcher wasn't looking at me but at her catcher. She nodded when she decided on the pitch she wanted, and then she wound up. It came belt high, but I swung low, anticipating the sinker, and it flew high and long, rattling the fence with a hit three feet off the ground. As the center fielder chased it, I ran for first. Gwennie came in easily for our seventh run. Coach Marge was serving as first base coach and gave me a victory swat on the butt. "Great job, Medley, great focus." I barely contained a grin as I removed my batting gloves and handed them to her. Cynthia came up to bat and—was that a nod in my direction? I nodded back, astonished, and set my right foot on the bag, letting my arms hang loose as I awaited the pitch. She turned to face the pitcher, who wiped her forehead with the back of her arm. The pitcher took a breath, set, and swung her arm.

Cynthia made it to third on an error by the Eagles' short stop. I swooped in home to give our team our eighth run. Breathless as I crossed homeplate, I slowed to a jog to return to the dugout, where everyone greeted me with grins and high fives. Ariela rattled the fence that walled us off from the bleachers. "You did great, kid," she said in a low voice.

"I miss playing with you," I said, holding my left hand up to the fence. She held her hand up against the fence where mine was, and we smiled huge smiles at one another.

Tiffany hit a soaring pop-up that the Eagles' pitcher caught easily for our third out. I put on my catcher's gear and trotted out to homeplate.

The Eagles got their groove back after the surprisingly poor defensive performance, scoring six runs in the bottom of the first. Once we got to the second inning, our runs were much harder-won, and by the bottom of the last inning, we were leading by one. I crouched into position. The Eagles' number three batter came up. I'd noticed at her previous at-bats that she liked to swing for high pitches, so I signaled to Cynthia to do a drop-pitch. She nodded and let one fly, fooling the batter just like I'd been fooled by the Eagles' pitcher. *Karma.* She swung for a strike. On the next pitch, a fast pitch, the batter made contact but got under it, and the ball soared high and dropped into left field where it landed in Rebecca Wilson's glove for the first out. Their next batter came up, and I signaled for Cynthia to use a rise ball. She did, and the batter who had made contact with everything hit low missed. The folks in the stands erupted. I signaled for a changeup next. The batter hit the ball foul for strike two. On the third pitch, I signaled for a fastpitch, which was Cynthia's strong suit. She let it fly, and the batter swung hard—a beat after the ball had landed in my glove. Our fans lost it, screaming and rattling the fence. Adrenaline pulsed through me. Victory tasted sweet in my mouth, but we weren't there yet.

The next batter stepped up, and it was the Eagles' pitcher. She stepped up to the plate. She had had a couple of

RBIs already; she didn't seem to be deterred by any pitch. I signaled for another fastpitch. Cynthia let it loose. The batter made contact with the ball—and hit it straight back at Cynthia's head. Cynthia ducked. The ball caught her on the side of the helmet. She dropped to the ground and lay still. I threw down my headgear and ran up to the mound as a hush swept through the stands.

"Cynthia, are you okay?" I said, fighting to keep my voice calm but firm. I put my hand in front of her mouth.

"She's breathing," I said to Coach Marge as she came up.

"She's not conscious," Coach said quietly after a quick assessment. "Someone call 911!" Coach called out.

"I'm on it," called the coach of the Eagles, hurrying out to the mound, phone in hand.

In a moment Cynthia's parents were kneeling next to her. Her father moved to take Cynthia's helmet off her head, but I put a hand on his chest to stop him.

"Please don't touch her," I said. "You're Mr. Marshall, right?"

He glared at me.

"I'm Medley."

"I know who you are," he said.

"Mr. Marshall, if she has any kind of injury from her fall, moving her could make things worse. The best we can do is wait for the paramedics."

Mr. Marshall's eyes narrowed. He looked angry. I maintained my composure. I had taken a Basic Life Support course two years ago after the little brother of one of my Little League teammates had begun choking on a peanut and no one knew what to do. He'd nearly died. The course had taught me that command was everything when acting as a first responder.

"Medley's right," Coach Marge said, putting her hand on my shoulder. "For now let's give Cynthia room to breathe."

Mr. Marshall and his wife stayed back. The umpires moved into crowd control, instructing everyone to get off the field. Coach Marge, Mr. and Mrs. Marshall, and I remained. When the umpires approached us, Coach Marge let them know we were going to stand next to her to keep her shaded. The sound of emergency sirens grew increasingly loud, and soon a fire truck and squad vehicle from Tempe Fire No. 3 arrived.

They parked and approached quickly, and soon they had Cynthia on a stretcher and were rolling her down the sidewalk to an ambulance that had just pulled up. Mr. and Mrs. Marshall went with her. After all of that, I turned and saw the coaches talking to the umpires.

Then the homeplate umpire called out: "Game!" I remembered then that pitchers were off-limits, and hitting one meant an automatic out. With that out, the Hummingbirds had won. Coach Marge and the coach of the Eagles shook hands. Stunned, I lined up with the other team. We clapped hands in silence. The Eagles' pitcher was red-faced and didn't make eye contact.

The victory felt hollow. We'd be going to the championship game next weekend, but would Cynthia be there? Would she even be okay? She was a jerk, but she didn't deserve this. And she was my best friend's girlfriend. I gasped, turning suddenly to look for Ariela. She was sitting alone in the bleachers. I began walking toward her, but Coach Marge called us into a huddle. Reluctantly, I turned back.

"Ladies, we won, but not the way any of us ever would

have wanted." Sniffles sounded around the team. Even I was teary-eyed. "I trust everyone will keep Cynthia's recovery in mind this week. She won't be playing next week, but we will, so Jennifer will be lead pitcher."

I made eye contact with Jennifer.

"Medley, I'd like to get you and Jennifer together this Thursday to practice together."

"Sure thing, Coach," we said in unison.

She gave us a tight smile.

"We've been fighting our way to the championship all season, but now we have even more on the line. Our teammate is hurt and won't be able to help us, so let's go out to win it for her."

Coach put her hand in the center, and the rest of put our hands in as well.

"For Cynthia," Coach said.

"For Cynthia," we shouted.

I walked over to Jennifer. "See you here, Thursday, regular time?"

She nodded and gave me a high-five.

I turned and looked again for Ariela. But she was already gone.

Mom and Dad came over and gave me hugs.

"I'm sorry about your friend, honey," Mom said.

"She's not... she's not my friend. But yeah. It sucks."

We walked down the long sidewalk that ran to the parking lot. Someone called my name, and I turned. It was Gwennie. "Nice job today, Medley," she said.

I waved in return. Next to her, a woman with long black hair, deep brown skin, and a colorful, flowing skirt looked back at me. Silver jewelry on her arms and hands glinted in the sun. Was that who I had seen earlier? I wondered yet again about my mother—and wondered now if Gwennie Lightfoot might know anything about her.

Don't be ridiculous, Medley, I thought as I turned and entered the parking lot. *The world isn't that small.*

Chapter 14

How is she doing?”

Ariela slammed her locker door shut and rested her forehead on the gray metal. She didn't answer for a moment. It was Monday morning, and we had about a minute left before the tardy bell would ring. I touched her shoulder, but she shrugged me off.

“What do you care?”

I felt as though the wind had been knocked out of me. I didn't know what to say. As I stood there, Ariela shook her head and pushed past me.

“Ar....” I stopped mid-name, remembering where I was. She walked away.

“Wait!” I called. Ariela ignored me. There were just seconds left before the next bell would ring. I cursed under my breath and attempted to push through the crowd, but Ariela had already disappeared. I let out a frustrated grunt and whipped around to head to my homeroom, and nearly collided with Charles. He had a smirk on his face as he blocked my way.

"Your boyfriend there dump you?"

"Out of my way, Charles," I said. He didn't move. I stepped toward the middle of the hall, but he stepped with me.

"Are you a complete dope? Move it!" And I gave him a shove. He landed on the floor, eyes wide. "You're going to regret that, bitch."

I hurried around him and slid into my seat just as the tardy bell rang. Mr. Irwin took attendance. Charles was absent. Partway through Channel 1, Mr. Brantley's voice came over the PA. "Mr. Irwin, would you please send Medley Blunt to the office, please?"

"She'll be right down," Mr. Irwin said. Twenty pairs of eyes turned in my direction as I stood, slid my backpack on, and exited the room. The empty, locker-lined hallway echoed with my footsteps.

When I reached the office, the school secretary pressed a button and announced my arrival. Mr. Brantley opened his office door and gestured for me to enter the room.

In his office, Charles sat in one of several chairs in front of Mr. Brantley's desk. Mr. Brantley asked me to sit down. I sat in the one farthest from Charles.

"Medley, I'd like to hear your version of what happened between you and Charles this morning."

"What do you mean, Mr. Brantley?" No way was I about to admit to anything.

"Mr. Bedlam here states that you assaulted him in the hallway just before the tardy bell. Is this true?"

"No, sir. 'Mr. Bedlam' was antagonizing me as he usually does, and this time he stood in my way as I attempted to get to homeroom in a timely fashion, so I helped him out of my way."

Mr. Brantley stared at me. "That's not how Mr. Bedlam tells it. According to him, you antagonized him and wouldn't leave him alone. He states he declined your advances, and you shoved him to the floor as a result."

"Are you freaking kidding me? You think I would want anything to do with... that?" My hand flew in Charles's direction.

"Keep that hand in your lap, Ms. Blunt. Assault is a serious business. We do not tolerate it in this school."

"He was preventing *me* from getting to homeroom on time."

"Mr. Bedlam states you've been pursuing him for a couple of months now, and you've lashed out several times. He states you grabbed him inappropriately during homeroom a few weeks ago."

"*Charles* grabbed *me*," I said, my voice growing loud.

"And yet you have never stated any such thing to anyone in authority. It sounds very much to me like you have been harassing Mr. Bedlam, and this harassment will not be allowed to continue. You will be placed on a three-day in school suspension and barred from any extracurricular school activities, unless...." He let the sentence dangle.

"Unless what?" I said in a shrill voice.

"Unless you issue Mr. Bedlam a written apology for your actions, as well as an apology for your complicity in the events at the St. Patrick's Day Sock Hop."

I gaped at Mr. Brantley.

"First of all, I will not now or ever apologize for something that I didn't do. Secondly, I have no idea what you're talking about regarding the Sock Hop. Thirdly, if you think you can get away with treating me like this, I will personally have words with the school board to see about having you removed on the grounds that you are the most incompetent man ever to work in this school district."

I stood. Mr. Brantley turned beet red, and Charles raised his eyebrows.

"You will sit down, Ms. Blunt, or you will face expulsion from this school."

"Try me," I said. And I walked out, slamming the door behind me.

Only when Mr. Brantley's door flew open did I begin to run.

Mr. Brantley's voice growled behind me, but it grew fainter and fainter as I gripped the straps of my backpack and barreled forward, only touching the pavement with my toes to reduce friction and increase speed, as all my coaches had taught me.

I was out of breath by the time I reached my street. I slowed to a walk and let myself in the house a minute later. Both my parents were gone, and I was alone. I dropped my backpack on the floor and poured a glass of chilled water from the fridge. I gulped it down and then poured another, which I brought with me to the office. The room was cool and dark compared to the rest of the house. I flipped on the computer and opened my journal.

Monday, May 9, 2016

Well, I'm screwed.

Yesterday, on the final pitch, the batter hit the ball squarely back at Cynthia and knocked her out. We won the game on that automatic out, but Cynthia's condition is a big question mark. I asked Ariela how she was doing this morning before homeroom, but she was mad at me. Then I turned to go to class, and Charles Freaking Bedlam got in my way and wouldn't let me by, so I shoved him. He reported me to the principal, who now says I'm on 3-day ISS, including suspension from extracurriculars, unless I write a written apology to Charles as well as an apology for my "complicity" in the events at the Sock Hop. He threatened to expel me if I walked out. I walked out, and then ran when Mr. Brantley tried to chase me down.

I'm sure my parents have been called by now. I just heard our phone ring, but I didn't answer it.

I'm totally screwed. This means I can't finish off my final piece of the year for the newspaper. After what happened yesterday, I didn't make it to the library anyway. I went home and watched tv for the rest of the day. I just wanted to block it all out.

I hate this school. I hate Charles. I hate that Ariela is mad at me. I hate that Cynthia is such a jerk that I get the stink-eye from Ariela for not liking her—it's not like I was the one who sent a softball flying into her skull. I hate that my parents can't get it together. I hate that my little brother is dead. I hate that he wasn't even my real brother. I hate that I'm this close to knowing who my bio-family is, but still worlds away. I hate that Mr. Brantley treats me and Ariela and all the other non-conformists like garbage and that he has so much power to *make us miserable. I hate that I don't know where I belong.*

I don't know what to do.

I could just leave it all behind. Run away. Go find my bio-mom. Make her be my mom again.

I could start fresh.

A new life—the life I should have had all along—is just a bike-ride away.

I stared at the computer screen as streams of tears ran down my face.

I saved my journal entry and shut down the computer. I went to my room to gather some of my things. I debated writing a note to leave my parents. In the end, I scratched out a message in one of my notebooks.

"Mom and Dad, I figured out who I really am. I'm leaving for the life I was supposed to have. I love you. Tell Aaron I'm sorry. -Medley"

And after locking the door, and leaving my key under the mat, I got on my bike and pedaled toward Price Road and my new life.

When I reached the museum, I parked my bike in the back out of sight, just in case anyone came looking. I walked around and tried the door, but it was locked. I knocked. I waited.

No answer.

I knocked again, brushing sweat off my forehead. *Maybe this wasn't such a good idea, Medley.*

Your name isn't Medley anymore, I chided myself.

I knocked one more time, but there was no answer, and no sound in the museum. Flustered and losing confidence by the second, I wandered around looking for another entrance. There was none.

What am I doing here?

I looked around. The reservation was flat apart from the mountains that rose up here and there in the distance. Just then, an elderly man opened the door to the museum.

"May I help you?" he asked kindly.

"Um...." I paused, not knowing what to say, and thinking it might not be wise to come right out and say what I was there for.

My face grew hot with embarrassment.

The man eyed me.

"Do you think I could borrow your phone?" I had left my phone behind, not wanting my parents to track me that way.

"I'm afraid I don't have a phone you could use here, but I think there are some payphones at the courthouse just down the street."

"Thank you for your help," I mumbled. The man didn't follow me.

I wandered onto a playground, where a couple of mothers were letting their young children play. I approached one of the moms.

"Excuse me, but I was wondering if I could borrow your phone. I left mine at home."

The woman eyed me. "Shouldn't you be in school right now?"

"I... I'm homeschooled," I said, reaching for a believable answer.

"There are phones at the courthouse," she said, and moved closer to her children, glancing back at me as she walked.

Strike two.

I wandered away from the playground and toward the visitor center. Whoever had designed these buildings had done a beautiful job. It seemed odd that such beautiful buildings would stand at the center of lands dotted with abandoned or dilapidated homes. A number of the homes were well-kept, but just as many weren't. It was strange to be here. It was so different from the neighborhood I grew up in, packed with homes that were all kept to a strict standard imposed by the housing association.

I entered the visitor center. A couple of payphones stood along one wall. I approached the main desk there and asked the receptionist if he could make change so I could make a phone call. He obliged with a smile, trading me a dollar for four quarters. Change in hand, I approached the payphones. The sticker on each phone indicated local calls cost fifty cents. *What a rip-off!*

I sighed and put two quarters in the slot after picking up the phone, but I couldn't think of any number to call. I hung up the phone and the quarters tumbled into the return tray. I pocketed them and exited the courthouse.

My stomach began to grumble, so I headed to the café for a bite. It wasn't quite ten o'clock. I chose a breakfast burrito and a bottle of soda, paid for both with some of the money I had stashed in my bag, and headed outside to sit at a table in the shade. I realized as I began to eat that I hadn't eaten this morning, or much last night, either—my stomach had been churning ever since the game. Now I ate ravenously. I polished off the burrito within minutes. Before long, I had to pee, so I returned to the café to use the bathroom. By the time I emerged, I felt better than I had in a day. The day no longer seemed grim, but hopeful.

I bought a bottle of water and returned to the park, where I sat in a corner on a bench by myself. Thoughts of my identity spilled swiftly into a notebook as I waited for the next chapter of my life to begin.

Chapter 15

As I waited, a number of families, all with skin and hair and eyes as dark as mine came through the park. I sketched some of them, wishing I had more than a blue pen to work with. My white parents would have been the outliers in this setting. The folks who came through weren't wearing what I thought of as traditional native dress—they were in t-shirts, jean shorts, and sneakers, by and large.

Despite the heat, chills covered my skin as I spied one little kid in khaki shorts and a PJ Masks t-shirt running around, screaming. The kid looked like my brother as I had dreamed him so many times in the last few weeks, but in reality, the kid could have been a boy or a girl. There was no way to tell. Ariela would have been tickled by the ambiguity.

Thinking of Ariela sent dread through me like daggers. Would she understand my departure? Surely she'd know where

I'd gone, so it wouldn't be like she couldn't find me if she really wanted to.

Will she tell my parents?

Surely she wouldn't. And maybe they wouldn't even ask her. If they did ask her, she could just say that we'd parted each other this morning on bad terms, and she didn't know anything. She could make her life easier by focusing on Cynthia and pretending like she knew nothing at all. And then I could live my new life, and she hers. And maybe we'd meet again someday, as grown-ups, when we weren't being bossed around by dingbats like Mr. Brantley.

When the sun hung overhead, I got up, put my things in my backpack, and hurried to the bike-rack. The seat was hot to the touch, so I opted to walk my bike over. As I was turning the corner around the museum, I caught sight of a police car with its lights on. An officer was standing at the front door with the elderly man I'd spoken to earlier. I gasped and stepped back. A minute later, I peered around the corner. The officer was getting into his car. The man had disappeared. I wheeled the bike around and tucked myself and the bike behind the museum, out of sight. I watched the police cruiser roll by moments later. The cruiser belonged to the reservation, though. Surely that exchange wouldn't have been about me. Would it?

I waited another couple of minutes and then returned to the entrance of the museum. I tried the door; it was unlocked this time. I entered. The midwife was back at the desk. The elderly man stood next to her. They both looked over.

"Wipismal," the midwife said, meeting my eyes with a soulful—or was it sorrowful?—gaze. "You shouldn't be here. You should be in school."

I shook my head. I wasn't about to be set aside. A lifetime of being displaced had made my resolve firm on that much. "I'm here to see my mother, and I'm not leaving until I do," I said, folding my arms.

She and the old man exchanged words I didn't understand. The elderly man looked at me and hurried into the room beyond the curtain. The midwife gestured for me to follow her.

Ten minutes later, I sat across from both of them, a jug of iced tea and a platter of cookies between us. The midwife poured herself a glass of iced tea and offered the jug to me. I poured myself a glass, set the jug to the side, and took a sip. It was strong and refreshing.

"Thank you for your hospitality."

"You are welcome."

I set the glass down, eager and fearful at the same time. A thousand questions crowded on the tip of my tongue. "Where is my mother?"

The midwife took a sip of tea and set it down. "She is not far."

"Why did she give me up?"

"I cannot speak for your mother."

My insides felt hollow. The hollowness began to fill with rage.

"How *could* she?"

"Wipismal, I am sorry. I do not have the answers you seek."

"Call her here, then."

Her eyes softened.

"Hohogimal," she said in a raised voice.

I heard the sound of a door click open. Footsteps grew louder. My voice caught in my throat. I turned.

And there she was, looking back at me. My flesh and blood. The woman who had given birth to me.

"Wipismal," she breathed.

Neither of us moved. I stared into her eyes, the very same eyes I had beheld in the mirror every day since I was old enough to look over the sink. In her eyes, I detected the same fire I saw in mine—and the same sorrow.

My chin quivered. Suddenly aware of myself, I stuck my chin out, clenching my jaw, hands balled up in fists at my sides.

"How could you?" I rasped.

"Sit," she said, nodding to the chair I occupied a moment ago.

"No." I folded my arms with my feet planted. "Tell me why you gave me up."

My mother looked at the midwife.

"Look at me!" I cried.

My mother's gaze returned to me. I could feel my legs begin to tremble from the tension of standing taut, waiting.

"I gave you up to save your life," she said in a low voice.

"You what?"

"Please... sit. I shall tell you the story." She gestured again to the chair next to me.

I sat.

"This story begins before you were born, nearly fourteen years ago."

The elderly man stood to excuse himself, but my mother gestured for him to stay. He touched her shoulder and offered her the chair he'd been sitting in. She took it. He leaned against the sink.

"I was not much older than you are now when a missionary came to the reservation. He was pale-skinned, but he dazzled everyone among us with his charm." She glanced at the midwife and continued.

"He created a youth club for the young people. He asked me to help more often than he asked the other kids, and I was happy to help. It felt good to be singled out.

"As we were preparing for our summer sweat lodge ceremony, this missionary seemed resistant to our tradition.

While he was amiable around the youth club, he spoke of his concerns to me privately. He said the sweat lodge ceremony was akin to sorcery. I attempted to persuade him otherwise. He seemed so kind in general, but when it came to our culture's ceremonies, he grew more and more worried, even angry.

"The night before the sweat lodge was supposed to take place, the missionary walked with me as I tried to help him understand the importance and goodness of the ceremony. We walked inside, and everything was set—the ground was raked smooth, the pit was prepared for the heated rocks, and the lodge itself was fully covered.

"The missionary said, 'This is a den of vipers! Only sin can come from this place!' And before I could protest, he kissed me. I tried to back away, but he blocked the entrance. He forced me to the ground. He was stronger than I was. He unzipped his pants. I was wearing a dress, and he pulled down my panties while he held my hands with his other hand. He pinned my body with his body. He whispered that if I screamed, I would burn. He said the only way to keep from going to hell was to act as the bride of Christ. He said he would plant his holy seed in me to purify this place, but only if I was obedient."

Tears lined her face, but my mother's face was detached, calm. My heart raced.

"That was the night you were conceived. The only way to protect you was never to tell anyone. The missionary went away a couple of weeks after the sweat lodge. After that we never heard from him again. I went away to my aunt's house for a year. When you were born, only my aunt knew." She nodded toward the midwife. My eyes grew wide.

"I was barely a woman. I could not take care of you. But I was too ashamed to tell anyone, and I made her swear that she would never tell, or I would have an abortion.

"When you were born, my aunt spirited you away. I never knew where she took you. She simply said they had taken you somewhere safe."

I looked at the midwife, my great aunt, but now she would not meet my eyes.

"Do you mean to tell me," I said, standing slowly and turning to my great-aunt, "that you let my mother's rape be covered up? That you ripped me away from my mother's arms and never told anyone?"

My mother stood and touched my arms, turning me toward her. "She did not rip you out of my arms. I let you go willingly. I could not care for you. I was not ready to be a mother. And I could not bear the humiliation of letting my rape be known. My aunt did as I asked. I wanted you to have a life— a life free from the shame of being the child of a rapist. I wanted you to have a life free from the dishonor that knowledge of the event would have brought upon our family."

I shook my head, my eyes glassy with tears. "You let your flesh and blood go. I had no idea who I was. I had no idea why I didn't look like my parents. They would never tell me anything. I ended up in a white neighborhood with a white family in white schools where I was made fun of and shunned for my skin color. I only found out the first inkling of who I was by accident. How long were you willing to let me live in ignorance?"

My mother's eyes fell. "I knew that if we ever met again, you would be full of questions, if not anger. I have spent my life regretting not being everything for you. Every day of my life, I have wished for your well-being, for your joy. I didn't dare hope that you would return to me, but here you are. As pained as I am to see your anguish and hurt, I am thrilled beyond my wildest dreams to see you here, to talk to you, to hear you, to look into your eyes as I did just after you were born. You are my greatest love and my greatest gift to the world."

I couldn't breathe.

My knees began to buckle.

My mother pulled me into her before I could fall, and she hugged me tightly. My mother. My mother who had been wronged. My mother who wanted me, but sent me away so I could live without dishonor. My mother who loved me. I hugged her back and sobbed. I could scarcely catch my breath. Waves of pain, powered by unknowing, rocked me. All that remained was this moment. I looked into my mother's face and saw myself reflected in her. She smiled and pressed her forehead against mine, nuzzling my nose.

"Come," she said, and she guided me gently to another room, where we sat together on an old couch. My great-aunt brought us hot black tea. We sipped it together, side by side.

"What do we do now?" I asked, my head cradled in my

mother's shoulder. A thousand questions still remained, but the immediate and long-term future remained uncertain. I needed to know where I stood.

"Does your family know where you are?"

I thought of my parents. By now they would have been contacted by the school. They might have come home and found my note. I thought of Mark, and the pain they endured in losing him. And now they were losing their only other child. Guilt grew thick, cramping my gut.

"They don't know. I ran away. Things all kind of fell apart. I… I don't think I can go back."

My mother turned and faced me, her face wrought with seriousness.

"If you do not let your parents know where you are, they will never stop seeking you. And if they find you here…."

"But I'm your daughter by blood. They can't take me from you."

"If it comes to legal action, you might very well be returned to me. But tell me—are you parents good to you? Do they love you?"

"Yes," I whispered.

"You do not know the pain of losing a child as I have. Please, let's contact them and let them know where you are. We can talk together. We can sort through this."

"I don't want to lose you," I hiccuped. Snot ran down my nose.

"You will never lose me again. I promise. I promise." And then my mother held me, humming a lullaby, a lullaby laced with my birth name.

After a while, sitting just like that with my birth mother, I became calm. Breaking the quiet gently, she said, "Would you like to talk to your family now?"

I nodded, and we walked into the kitchen together, where my great-aunt awaited us with a phone.

Chapter 16

Mom, it's me. I'm okay."

After a minute or two of hysteria from her end of the phonecall, I managed to explain where I was.

"You're where?"

"On the reservation. With my bio-mom."

The line went silent for so long that I wasn't sure we were still connected. I looked at the phone and held it back to my ear.

"Hello?"

"Tell me exactly where you are and we'll come meet you," Mom said. "And we'll call off the search party on the way."

I told her the name of the museum so she could look it up on her maps app. I also told her that Ariela had been there with me before.

"He *what*?"

My parents pulled into the parking lot within fifteen

minutes. Ariela and her parents were right behind them. By that time the sun was falling low in the sky.

My great-aunt ushered everyone inside to the living room, where my mother was pulling in extra chairs so everyone could sit down. With the eight of us, it was a tight fit. Once we were all sitting, silence took hold.

My bio-mom broke the silence. "I'd like to introduce myself. I'm Hohogimal. I'm Medley's biological mother." *Guess that clears that up.*

I talked next. "Everyone knows me. Medley is the name I go by, but Wipismal is the name I was given at birth."

My mom and dad went next. "I'm Melissa Blunt, Medley's adoptive mom," Mom said.

"I'm Brian Blunt, Medley's adoptive dad."

"I'm Daniel Spieler, Aaron's father."

"I'm Yizkah Spieler, Aaron's mother."

"And I'm Ariela, also known as Aaron."

Ariela's parents and mine turned and gaped at her. Ariela turned to her parents, then turned briefly to me.

"Sorry to steal your thunder, Medley. But while we're

revealing all, I want everyone in this room to know something I've known for a long time. I'm transgender. I am a girl. Medley's known for a while now."

"She what?!" My parents and hers turned to look at me. I looked at them and shrugged.

"I told Medley a few months ago. I knew she wouldn't judge me. She's my best friend, and she's always had my back."

Ariela looked at me then with piercing eyes, holding a hand to her heart. I held a hand up to mine.

"Anyway, just thought you all should know. Figured this was as good a time as any. Back to you, Medley."

I snorted. Ariela grinned through teary eyes.

My bio-mom patted my knee and urged me to explain how I came to be here.

I took a deep breath. "I have long wondered where I came from, since I clearly look nothing like my parents. I've known for a long time that I'm adopted, but I didn't know much more to the story than that. I was in my parents' office one day a few weeks back, and I found my birth certificate. I took it as a clue to who I was, and I dragged Ariela out with me to come here with the hope of finding out something about who I was."

The eyes of all the grown-ups turned to Ariela. I continued.

"I met the woman who worked at the main desk here. She knew who I was. She told me she was the midwife at my birth. And then this woman walked in," I nodded at my biological mother, "and I realized I looked exactly like her, and I ran out.

"Long story short, things kinda fell apart, and I couldn't stand being where I was anymore. Not because of you, Mom and Dad," I hurried to say, "but just stuff at school, and I thought Ariela hated my guts, and I was feeling really low. So I came up here this morning and waited till the museum opened. I found my bio-mother here, and she told me the story of how I ended up being adopted. Her side of it, that is."

The room was suddenly full of an uncomfortable silence.

"And now here we all are," I said.

"Medley, we'd like to take you home now," my dad said in a hoarse voice.

"No," I said.

I ignored the expressions on my parents' faces. I still

didn't have all the answers.

"I want to know how you ended up adopting me," I said.

Mom and Dad exchanged looks.

"It was my doing," my great-aunt said.

I turned to her, surprised.

"As a midwife, I knew that there were numerous safe places I could take you to. I knew someone who worked at a fire station in Tempe. I left you at the doors to the firehouse. As it happened, your mom and dad had been trying to have a baby for a while, and when they found out you needed a home...."

"We didn't hesitate, Medley," Mom said.

"And who was the person who facilitated all this?"

My parents exchanged looks with my great-aunt.

"She's the widow of the firefighter who found you," Mom said.

"What's her name?"

"Lila Hopley," my great-uncle said.

"You mean... Ms. Hopley? The school counselor?"

"Yes," Dad said.

Son of a freaking gun.

"Are you ready, Medley?" Mom asked.

"What? No. Hang on. Just hang on," I said. "This is my life we're talking about now. I'm not a possession you can simply claim and take home with you. I'm thirteen years old, and I deserve a say."

"Medley," Dad began, but I held up my hand.

"Mom and Dad, I love you. You are my family. But so is this woman. And so is this woman." I gestured to my bio-mom and great-aunt. "I want to know who I am, not just be who I've always been told to be."

"What are you saying, Medley?" Ariela asked quietly.

I blew out a breath. "I'm saying that now that I've had a taste of where I came from, I want to taste more. I want the whole freaking smorgasbord. I want to know my birth mother. I want to learn about my roots, my culture, everything. I need to know. There's so much to catch up on."

"But honey, you have a life in Tempe."

"Well, I don't know if Mr. Brantley informed you today, but he threatened me with three days of in-school-suspension this morning, complete with suspension of all school extracurriculars, if I didn't write a written apology to a boy who has been harassing me for months. He also expected me to write an apology for my 'complicity' in the events at the St. Patrick's Day Sock Hop, whatever that means."

"He what?" Dad said, his voice rising.

"Yeah. True story. I have no interest in going back there."

"Me, neither, truth be told," Ariela said. "That guy is a poster-boy for homophobia. No way is he going to let me be me once I come out at school. Which I intend to do tomorrow, by the way."

"What about Cynthia?" I asked.

"She knows. I went to see her at the hospital right after school."

"Really?" I squeaked.

"Really. I probably should've waited. I thought she was going to pass out again when I told her. But she knows. And she said she likes me, the real me, not just the me I put on for everyone else to see. So I guess we're good," Ariela said.

Holy crap. Anything else?

"Medley," Mom said. I looked at my adoptive mom, who

looked as though she was about two inches from disaster. "Medley, I get what you're saying and your feelings make sense to me. But call me selfish: I don't want to lose you. I've already lost one child this year. Please don't leave us. Please."

Suddenly I was no longer the child. I was the decision-maker, the one in authority, the one on whom the fate of all rested. I stood, crossed the room, and knelt at her feet. She tousled my hair, her eyes wet and desperate.

"Mom, I will always be your baby. I'm just going to be someone else's baby, too." I turned to my bio-mom and held out my arm. My bio-mom walked over and knelt next to me, our sides touching, her arm wrapped around my waist.

"We'll figure out how to make this work," I said. "I love all of you, and I want to be with all of you. We'll figure it out. But I'm going to need you, all of you, to hear me. And I guess we'll all need to be flexible."

The remainder of the week was a blur. I returned to Mom and Dad's house, with promises on both sides that I could begin spending weekends with my bio-mom as soon as school was out. I was referring to her now as Zhay, which was my best approximation for the word for "mother" in my mother's tongue.

Ariela did indeed come out. She wrote "My name is Ariela. Nice to meet you" in purple, glittery puffpaint on a white t-shirt and wore it to school on Tuesday. The look on Mr. Brantley's face—oh, the look on his face. But he couldn't say much at all, because the Spielers and my parents all descended on his office at once that morning to let him know exactly what was what, complete with threats to take matters to the school board if needed. By the end of the day, written notes from him and Charles landed in my hands, via Ms. Feliz, who was delighted to welcome me into her room at the end of the day to let me type up my final piece of the year for the school paper. I even got to call my mother for clarification on details regarding sweat lodge ceremonies, including the misappropriation of them by non-native peoples and the dangers thereof. *Because no article of mine would be complete without taking it in a completely unconventional direction. So gauche.*

Jennifer Perez and I did meet up Thursday under the

guidance of Coach Marge, and we got a nice rhythm down. Cynthia came out to cheer us on game day—dressed in uniform and all—and it turned out that Jennifer, in addition to being a swell Little League shortstop, is a mighty fine fast-pitch softball pitcher. We squeaked out a championship win and held Cynthia on our shoulders afterward so she could hold our trophy high. Ariela took the opportunity to announce the she'd be joining the team for fall ball, and Cynthia asked to be set on the ground so she could kiss her right there in front of everyone.

Before long, the school-year was over, and I was heading out for my first weekend with Zhay. As it happened, that weekend was the weekend before the sweat lodge ceremony. Zhay took me around the complex where she introduced me to everyone she knew as "Wipismal, my long-lost daughter." She said no more than that, and neither did I. Everyone welcomed me, and I scrambled to take notes on everyone I met in a little notebook I had tucked in my pocket so I could remember them next time I saw them.

The next weekend, my parents dropped me off, kissing me goodbye before I joined Zhay to prepare for the sweat lodge ceremony. Folks from the community would take turns throughout the night participating in the sweat. Zhay and I heated rocks together for the beginning of the sweat, and then transported them carefully to the pit. Others would heat additional rocks, but we were the ones to begin the ceremony. I clasped her hands outside the lodge before the ceremony started.

"Thank you for letting me be here with you, Zhay. Are you sure... are you sure this is okay?"

Zhay smiled at me, brushing a stray lock of hair behind my ear. "Wipismal, what happened to me those years ago was the worst thing that's ever happened to me. But it also brought about the best thing that's ever happened to me: you. The memory of that awful night can never be greater than what I was able to bring forth from it. The sweat lodge is now, has always been, and will always be sacred to me. It is even more so now that I can share it with you.

"Do you want to know what your name means?" she asked me, as we were welcoming people into the lodge.

"Of course," I said.

"It means 'hummingbird.' Hummingbirds are rather defensive, especially when it comes to their family, but they also migrate, helping flowers bloom wherever they grow. And, of course, they bring their own bright beauty to every place they dwell." I nodded, wondering how much of Ms. Hopley's knowledge of hummingbirds had come from my bio-family.

I smiled at the colorful woman who had brought new life to the world from tragedy, the woman who had guarded her own territory carefully while bringing her own brightness to it, in her own way, on her own terms. As we settled into the sweat lodge, the smell of fire, sweat, smoke, and spice surrounding us, I gazed at the woman who was my mirror image. She gazed back, and I couldn't help but laugh with delight—and she laughed right along with me.

ACKNOWLEDGEMENTS

It took five years to bring this story to birth. I had many competent and encouraging doulas along the way. I am grateful to John Burns for giving me an excuse to finish the first full draft by agreeing to offer feedback on it upon completion. This book likely wouldn't exist without him. I am also grateful to Andrea Dobbins for helping me understand the story I was trying to tell, for offering relentless encouragement, and for capturing the story's arc in the form of a book cover. I am grateful to Larissa Coleman who read through the early chapters as I was writing them and urged me to keep going, and also to Keeley Bruner for bearing witness to the life-changing revelation that I wanted to be a full-time (rather than occasional) novelist.

I am grateful to my children, Anastasia and Miriam, who have grown from wee sprites to vivacious, world-changing little ladies as this book has matured. Medley mirrors them. I am also grateful to my husband, Michael. Medley wouldn't have learned to play ball without him.

M.K.A.

ABOUT THE AUTHOR

After a childhood immersed in characters found on the page, M. Kate Allen now spends her adult life weaving magical tales of her own. She can be found tromping around central Arizona on the hunt for a glorious sunset, a fine bridge, a quirky house, a mouthwatering taco, or a cup of coffee.

M. Kate Allen lives with her family in Tempe, Arizona.